Colter's pistol roared once again, and Dan fell to his knees, a bullet through the middle of his forehead. He crumpled over as Colter brought his pistol down with great force atop Jed's head, knocking him cold. Jed folded into a heap.

Colter, with a calm smoothness, reached down and picked up the money. He stuffed some in Jed's shirt, then removed Jed's pistol from its holster. He placed his own pistol in Jed's right hand, and holstered Jed's pistol on his own gunbelt. He walked out the back of the barn and outside to his waiting horse. Smoke wove lazy patterns over the dead men, hanging over them like some wispy wraith in the dead silence.

Three men lay dead, and Jed, with a cracked skull, sank deeper into darkness, blood seeping from a deep gash in his head, trickling onto the straw and earth of the barn, forming into a bright crimson pool.

Jory Sherman

ABILENE GUN DOWN

POCKET STAR BOOKS
NEW YORK LONDON TORONTO SYDNEY

An *Original* Publication of POCKET BOOKS

A Pocket Star Book published by
POCKET BOOKS, a division of Simon & Schuster Inc.
1230 Avenue of the Americas, New York, NY 10020

Copyright © 2004 by Jory Sherman

ISBN: 0-7434-7700-6

First Pocket Books printing July 2004

10 9 8 7 6 5 4 3 2 1

Cover design by Jessie Sanchez
Cover illustration by George Bush
Interior design by Davina Mock

Manufactured in the United States of America

For information regarding special discounts for bulk purchases, please contact Simon & Schuster Special Sales at 1-800-456-6798 or business@simonandschuster.com

In memory of Charley Perlberg,
teacher, friend, and writer

ABILENE
GUN
DOWN

CHAPTER

1

THE WESTERN SKY WAS A MOIL OF GAUDY COLORS, A smear of softly blazing crimson, mingled with smudges of violet and purple, streaked with dazzling, vibrant gold bleeding through spatters of yellow and orange, as if some mad painter had squeezed tubes of oil paint on a palette and then tried to wipe it clean with a scarlet cloth.

The cattle, three hundred head of them, were strung out for a quarter of a mile or more under a faint pall of dust that seemed to follow them as if the grit were composed of lead filings and their backs were magnetized.

The dust spooled out from behind the herd, coating Jed Brand with dust, the fine grains seeping through the faded blue bandanna covering his nose and mouth, clinging to the sweat stains under his arms and on the front of his sun bleached chambray shirt. He had choked on that stinging, blasting dust for fifteen mile or more because it was his turn that day to ride drag while his brother Dan rode point. Silas Colter, the bastard, held the flanks with his cutting horse, well out of the dust and heat generated by the cattle. Colter rode well out so he could see both sides and if a cow strayed, he could be there with his horse under him and drive the cow back into the herd.

But by then, after weeks of being driven north, the herd was mite near trained. None of the longhorns strayed unless they were near water and hadn't drunk in a while, or if the leaders stirred up a sidewinder or two. Jed felt some pride about that. He and his brother had taken over as drovers in Waco after others had driven them up from deep in the Rio Grande Valley. That old mossy-horned cow in the lead, up there with Dan, had to break in two new drovers. She was as cranky as a Missouri mule until Jed and Dan had showed her who was boss. She kept wanting to turn around and head south, but now she had her wet nose to the wind and if she'd been bridled, she would have the bit in her teeth.

Behind him, a mile or so maybe, there was a youngster bringing up the remuda, a Mexican boy named Julio Cardoza whom Colter had picked up at Jed's suggestion. Julio knew horses and loved them so much he slept with them. Dan was always kidding Julio about being half horse, but Julio never minded that. It was as if he were proud to be joked about in that way.

"I am half horse," Julio always said. "But you do not say which half, the front or the back."

"Dan's the butt half," Jed told Julio.

And Cardoza always laughed at that.

He said he didn't really know how old he was, but thought he might have sixteen years. As he put it, *"Creo que yo tengo diez y seis anos."* Spanish is different than English. They say they have sixteen years. They have hunger. They have thirst. Jed spoke Spanish better than Dan did and he thought that was because he could think better in the language than his younger brother. It was a constant quarrel between them.

"What the hell do you want to speak Spanish for, Jed? You ain't no Mexican," Dan would say.

"Danny, you always think the Mexicans in Waco are talking about you behind your back. You always call what they say a lot of jabberin'. But if you understood their language, you'd know they weren't talking about you."

"What are they talking about?"

"Girls," Jed would say. "And money."

"Because they don't have neither."

"That's right, Danny. And, neither do we."

They would laugh after that, and the argument would be forgotten.

Cardoza was an orphan. Colter hadn't wanted to hire him on, but Jed convinced him that they'd wear out horses on such a long drive, from Waco up to Abilene in Kansas, and they needed a remuda and Julio was the best horse wrangler around those parts. After a few days on the trail, Colter stopped his grumbling about having a boy doing a man's work. He and Julio didn't get along, but as Jed said, "Ain't nobody can get along with Colter. The man's got a mean streak in him a mile wide and two miles deep," he told Dan.

"He may be plumb mean," Dan said, "but he ain't got a sense of humor."

Which was true, Jed thought, as he wondered when Colter was going to call a halt. They were at least another day's drive from Abilene and the prairie was going to be dark as a coal bin once that sun was down and they all had tired on them like a worn-out overcoat.

Jed motioned to Colter, beckoning him to ride over for a talk.

Colter turned his horse in a tight circle and gamboled back to the rear of the herd. He was a lean whip of a man with a sharp, chiseled face, pale blue eyes that were as vacant as the inside of a seashell and with that same hollow look to them. They were eyes a man couldn't read. Eyes most men wouldn't want to read.

His white duster flapped behind him as he broke into a gallop and rode closer, giving him the look, through the dust, of a bony wraith risen from some long-forgotten boot hill.

"What you got in your craw, Brand?" Colter growled as he rode up alongside Jed. His duster collapsed like a sheet on a windless clothesline. Half of a cheroot sprouted from his mouth, the end of it unlit. Colter never smoked them, he just chewed them into pulp and spat out the last chunk like a prune pit.

"Ain't you goin' to bed this herd down, Colter, or are you aimin' to run us all by moonlight?"

"You just keep your pecker in your pants, Jed. They's a crick 'bout a mile ahead and it's got long grass on both sides. We ain't but another day's short ride from Abilene once we cross that little ol' crick."

"You know, Silas," Brand said, "there just might be a heart beating in that scrawny chest of yours, after all. I was beginning to give up all hope of ever stopping to rest."

"Son, I guarantee them cattle will know when to stop long before you do. Once we hit that crick, they'll line up like children at a candy store window and your day's work'll be almost done."

Jed laughed, despite his weariness and Colter's abrasive manner. The man was like a burr under the saddle blanket at times. Most of the time, Jed thought. There was just something not right about Colter, as if he were just a half inch off of plumb. Dan hadn't complained much because he was so easygoing, but Colter positively rubbed Jed the wrong way, always pushing, pushing, to get the cattle up and moving early every morning, and holding them to the trail way too long, until a man's muscles were kinked up like a sackful of rusted chains, and Jed's temper was as short as the stub of cigar in Colter's mouth at the end of every blamed day. Maybe the man was in a hurry, but it sure as hell wasn't doing the cattle any good. They were starting to lose pounds and who in hell wanted to buy a bunch of skinny cattle?

Colter kept his eye on the herd all the time he was talking and when one of the cows started breaking from the herd, he slapped leather reins across his horse's rump and put spurs to its flanks. He wheeled the horse in a tight turn and galloped off.

Brand thought Colter was ever quick to keep the herd together and he admired him for that. They hadn't lost but two head the whole drive. One steer broke its leg in a gopher hole and had to be shot. Dan dressed it out and they cooked the choice parts until the meat turned rancid, so it wasn't a total loss. The other cow had fallen into a ravine and broken its neck. That one, too, died from a merciful bullet to its heart and was left for the wolves and coyotes.

Colter's horse cut the stray cow back into the herd as neatly as a man might slip a deuce back into a deck of playing cards. It was something to watch and Jed gave the man credit as a horseman.

The cattle in the vanguard began bawling when they drew near the creek. Their cries wafted back to Jed's ears and perked him up. Seconds later, Colter rode up with his latest orders.

"Bunch 'em up," he said.

Brand and Colter took off their hats and began ragging the cattle at the rear of the herd. They both yelled and the cattle picked up speed, running into the animals ahead of them so that the line swelled and fattened, bulging out on both flanks. Soon the whole herd was running toward the creek and Jed hauled in on the reins, slowing his horse. Colter did the same.

Jed could smell the water, feel the subtle shift in temperature.

"That'll hold 'em for a while," Colter said, riding up alongside Brand. "When they're finished watering, we'll cross 'em over and bed 'em down. I'll ride herd the first shift. You and Dan can draw straws to divide up the rest of the night."

"Think you can nighthawk this herd all by yourself, Silas?" Jed never missed an opportunity to goad Colter, just to see what was under the man's hard skin.

"Sonny, I been singin' to beeves longer'n you been alive. And when I nighthawk, they sleep like babes in a manger."

"Silas, you're not that much older'n I am and I'm twenty-two. I cut my teeth on a cow's teat."

"Well, I cut mine on a bull's balls and I was born with bowed legs, Brand."

The banter stopped when they reached the creek as the far clouds in the western sky began to turn to ash, leaving a solemn dark bruise on the horizon. The cattle were lined up along the creek, some striking the water with their hooves to splash water into their mouths, others lapping up gouts of water with rapid flicks of their parched tongues.

Jed slid his hat back from his forehead and turned his horse upstream. It was thirsty, too, and he needed to drink and fill his canteen before morning.

He looked back over his shoulder and saw Cardoza and the remuda coming up fast, the horses, having smelled water, running at a weary gallop. Jed took off his hat and waved a greeting to Julio, then clucked to his horse and rode up to water that didn't have a cow slobbering in it.

Dan was already there, flat on his stomach, sucking water into his mouth. He looked up as his brother dismounted and walked toward him, leading his horse.

"Boy, oh boy, Abilene tomorrow, Jed. I can take me a bath and put on some flower water and find me a pretty girl."

"Don't count your chicks before they break the shells with their pippins, Danny. Colter will find fourteen reasons not to pay us when we deliver this herd, and he'll have another half dozen orders to give us before we can shuck out of these dust-infested duds. You mark my words."

"Aw, Jed, you spoil everything. Colter's all right. He'll do right by us."

Jed lay down beside his brother and put his canteen into the water. He heard it gurgle as water fought to flow into its spout.

"I'm not so sure, Danny. Like I said. I don't trust the man as far as I can throw my saddle bronc."

The sky turned dark and the night came on with the suddenness of a shroud thrown over a corpse.

CHAPTER

2

JED DIDN'T LIKE IT, BUT COLTER SET THE RULES. While he, Colter, and Dan were eating a cold supper of beans, hardtack, and beef jerky, Julio had to watch the herd. He always ate last, and no amount of arguing with Colter had changed it since they left Waco.

The only thing on the fire was a pot boiling Arbuckle's coffee and, from experience, Jed knew it was strong enough to float a ten-penny nail. That was another thing. Colter always made the coffee, and he drank most of it himself. Jed used it to clear the dust out of his throat at night and the night phlegm out in the morning.

"Pretty fair grub," Dan said, as he shoveled beans and hardtack into his maw.

"If you like hog slop with sand in it." Jed chewed the jerky with measured bites, the scowl on his face plainly lit by the firelight.

"All you do is gripe, Jed," Colter said. "You think the world owes you a clean bunk and three squares a day? Huh? Be glad for what you got, son."

"I swear we drove fifteen miles today," Jed said. "Nothing would taste real good after all that dust and wear on my britches."

"More like ten mile," Colter said. "Anyways, we got no more'n eight to go until we hit McCoy's at Abilene."

"What's McCoy's?" Dan asked.

"The stockyards," Colter said. "Which reminds me. Jed, you bein' the oldest, I want you to drive 'em in and get the money from the buyer. I'll be in later. I got some business to take care of first."

Jed stopped chewing the tough leather in his mouth. "What?"

"You heard me. You'll collect the money for the herd and when I get it, I'll pay you off. I'll give you further instructions in the morning before we set out."

Jed sat there, staring at Colter. But Colter turned away from him, tossed his plate of leftovers to one side and got up to relieve Cardoza and take his turn as nighthawk. Dan and Jed watched him go without saying a word. Dan's fork clinked against his pewter plate as he cleaned up the last of his beans.

"He'll be back for his coffee," Jed said. "But he's pulling something, Danny. This deal has a smell to it I don't like."

"Aw, Jed, you always look on the bad side. Who cares? We'll get our money and never see Silas Colter again."

"Why isn't he going in to collect the money? That's all the man thinks about. Money. There's something fishy about all this."

"I don't see nothin' fishy about it. The man has things to do. He's just tryin' to do the best he can."

"There's something mighty peculiar about Silas, Danny. I keep wonderin' why his other drovers quit back in Waco. I just don't trust him."

"Well, we need the money and tomorrow he'll pay us. Ma's countin' on us and that money, you know?"

"I know, Danny. I've just got this itchy feeling under my skin that Colter's trying to get away with something and we're caught right in the middle."

Dan laughed and there was an underlying nervousness in his tinny cackle.

"You know," Dan said, to change the subject, "we heard back home how Kansas was flat as a pancake. Did you notice?"

"Notice what?"

"It ain't flat as a pancake, Jed. It's plumb flatter than a pancake."

Despite himself, Jed laughed, and the tension was broken. For the moment.

A few minutes later, Cardoza rode in while Jed and Dan were laying out their bedrolls.

"The horses are in the hobbles," he said, a grin on his face. "They are *muy cansado, como yo.*"

"Well, we're all tired, Julio," Jed told him. "Me, Dan, the cattle, our horses."

"Es verdad."

Cardoza poured a cup of coffee.

"Julio, you don't drink coffee," Jed said.

"This is for Mr. Colter. He say to bring him the cup."

"The man's a slavedriver," Jed said, drawing his saddle up to the head of his bedroll. "I hope he burns his tongue."

Dan fell asleep as soon as he lay down on his bedroll. Jed lay on his back, staring up at the stars strewn across the velvety heavens. When he turned and looked at the flickering fire, sleep overcame him. But before he dropped off, he wondered why Julio hadn't returned and eaten his supper.

CHAPTER

3

COLTER AWAKENED DAN FOR THE NEXT WATCH. DAN rode out to find the herd well bedded down and most of the cattle asleep. When he figured it was around 2:00 A.M., he woke his brother for the last watch.

Jed put on his hat, grabbed up his rifle, and saddled one of the horses in the remuda, Jubal, figuring to ride the gelding into Abilene. When he walked back to camp, he saw that Dan was already fast asleep. He saw Colter, lying on his back, snoring softly. But there was no sign of Julio. The man hadn't laid out his bedroll, evidently, at least not with them. Jed wondered if he had chosen to sleep elsewhere.

He shrugged and mounted Jubal, still half asleep in the chill night air.

"Crazy Mexican," he muttered under his breath, and rode off to tend to the herd. He listened to the lyrical songs of coyotes far off in the distance and then the trilling died out in a series of barking yaps and he was left in the silence of the night, dozing as he rode his circuit.

By the time the sun began etching the eastern horizon with pale fingers of cream light, the ground was glistening with fresh dew and Jed rode back into camp, fairly rested and alert. There was no sign of Julio Cardoza. Colter was up and relieving himself, while Dan was sitting up, his head down, trying to shake off his sleepiness.

"Dan, better get cracking," Jed said.

"I'm up," Dan moaned, his voice low in his throat.

Jed laughed. He swung down from Jubal and ground-tied him as he walked over to the small fire and hefted the pot. It was full of water but had not yet begun to steam.

"Coffee'll be ready in a few minutes," Colter said, buttoning up his trousers. "Herd all right?"

"Where in hell is Julio?" Jed asked.

"You askin' me?" Colter said.

"Who else? He rode out to bring you coffee last night. Haven't seen hair nor hide of him since."

"He brought the coffee and walked back here, I thought."

"Dan? Did you see Julio come back?"

"Naw. I fell asleep before you did, Jed." Dan rose up from his bedroll and ran dry fingers through his damp hair. He ran his hand over his beard. It had been stippling his face ever since they left Baxter Springs and was starting to curl into wool.

"That doesn't make any sense," Jed said. "Maybe we'd better look for him. I don't see his bedroll. Maybe he slept out where he hobbled the horses."

"I think he prefers horses to people," Colter said, as the coffeepot began steaming. "Why don't you ride over and take a look? You know where the horses are."

"I'll do just that," Jed said, scowling at Colter. "Since you don't seem to be worried much."

"I've got other things on my mind this morning." Colter picked up his tin cup and poured coffee into it. "Like some coffee, for one thing."

Jed snorted and rode off to where Julio had hobbled the small remuda of six horses, plus his own. Dan was pouring coffee into his cup when Jed left and rode over a small rise upstream where he had last seen the horses when he saddled up Jubal.

The horses were all there, including Julio's mare, Chiquita. She was still saddled, and Julio's bedroll was still tied on behind the cantle, the leather thongs still tightly knotted. Puzzled, Jed rode over and checked more closely. He tilted his hat back and scratched a spot just above his left temple. Julio had never returned to unsaddle the mare, that was plain to see. Jed realigned his hat and looked around as if Julio might come strolling up from that empty plain that surrounded him.

"Julio," Jed called, a rasp in his throat as dry as parched cornhusks.

There was no answer. Jed rode around, looking at the ground for boot tracks. There were some, but not enough. Just those of Julio leaving the remuda and walking to camp. Going, not coming back. Jed felt a flurry of moths in his stomach, the first pangs of fear. Fear not for himself, but for Julio. He knew Julio was not coming back. But where was he? Where had he gone? The fluttering in his stomach subsided and was replaced by something else, a hard anger, balling up inside him like a fist of iron.

Jed rode back to camp. Dan was drinking coffee with Colter. Both of them looked up at him as if he were someone they had never seen before. Jed dismounted, picked up his cup from near his bedroll and poured coffee into it. Then he set the cup down near the fire and walked over to Colter.

"Well, did you find Cardoza?" Colter asked.

"You know damned well I didn't find him, Silas."

"What in the name of Mildred's off-ox are you talking about, Brand?"

"I mean you were the last person to see Julio last night. After he gave you your damned coffee, he never came back. Chiquita's still under saddle and his bedroll is still tied down tight."

"Where's old Julio?" Dan asked, a dumbfounded expression on his face.

"Ask Silas there, Danny."

"Ask all you want, Dan," Colter said. "I don't know where that dumb Mexican wandered off to. And I don't give a damn."

"Well, maybe we could look for him," Dan said.

Colter doused his coffee into the fire. He shot Dan a withering look that made Dan turn his head away from Colter.

"Saddle up, Dan. We've got to get this herd moving and we're a man short. Jed, you'll have to wrangle those horses after we get the cows headed out, so don't dawdle none."

"Colter, I'm just about out of patience with you. You're responsible for Julio and I say we look for him. He didn't just wander off."

"There's only one man in charge here, Brand. And that's me. If we spot Cardoza along the way to Abilene, we'll pick him up. Otherwise, he's just another lost stray as far as I'm concerned. There's money on the hoof here and I mean to cash it in."

"You keep pushing me, Colter, and that's not all you'll cash in," Jed said.

"Make your play, Brand. Or shut up."

"Jed, don't go doin' nothin' hotheaded now, hear?" Dan said.

Colter threw his tin cup down on the ground and turned to brace himself, one hand floating just above the butt of his Colt. The cup rattled against some pebbles and then it grew quiet as Jed squared off.

"You call it, Colter," Jed said, his right hand sliding through the air toward his own pistol. "Maybe now's the time we see things come to a head between us."

"Jed, no," Dan said, starting toward his brother. "Don't be a fool. Think of our poor mama back in Waco."

"Yeah, maybe you'd better think of a lot of things, Brand, before you go for that six-gun on your belt. I'm game to go either way. You want boot hill, I'll give it to you, son."

"Stop calling me son, Colter," Jed said. "I ain't no kin to you."

"Your choice, Jed. Walk away and I'll forget this incident. Make your play and I'll punch your ticket."

Dan grabbed his brother and held both of his arms. He looked into Jed's eyes, pleading with him. "Jed, just calm down. There ain't no call to get yourself killed. Not over no Mexican."

Jed lifted an arm and swept his brother away. But he didn't go for his gun.

"Colter," he said, "I'm fed up with you, but we're just about to part company anyway. We'll get your herd up and running, but stay the hell out of my way until you pay us off in Abilene."

"Fair enough, Brand. Which reminds me. As I told you last night, I can't go into McCoy's with you. You and Dan take the herd in and you'll be met by a man named Malcolm Trent, or one of his agents. It's cash on the barrelhead, fifteen dollars a head. Just wait for me in the sale barn there and I'll pay you boys off and we can all have a drink on me at the Drover's Cottage."

"We'll do 'er, Mr. Colter," Dan said. "Whatever you say, boss."

Jed started to say something, but thought better of it. He nodded to Colter, who reached down, picked up his coffee cup and walked toward his bedroll. He put the cup inside it and rolled it up, hefted his saddle and bridle over his shoulder and walked toward the remuda.

"Dan, will you empty that pot and pack it for me?" Colter said as he passed the two men.

"Sure, Mr. Colter. I'll be right with you."

The Brand brothers watched Colter until he disappeared over the rise.

"Jed, you almost got us both killed. Take it easy, will you? Ma always said your hot temper would get you into trouble one day."

"Dan, you haven't even seen my temper yet. I just wanted to see how far Colter would go. And now I know."

"Yeah, he'd kill you as soon as look at you, if you press him."

"True, and it tells me something else, too, Danny."

"What's that?"

"Colter doesn't give a damn about you or me. And I think he knows a hell of a lot more about Julio than he's letting on."

"You don't know that, Jed. Why would he want to hurt little old Julio? Julio never hurt a dadblamed fly."

"That's what worries me, Danny."

Dan and Jed got the lead cows moving and, along with Colter, ran in the rest of the herd. Jed rode back and roped up the remuda so he could lead them and not have to worry about any of them running off. He used a long lead rope in case he had to drop it to chase cows. All the time, he was looking everywhere for some sign of Julio Cardoza. But somewhere in the deepest pit of his mind, he knew he would never see him again. A man like Julio didn't just disappear off the face of the earth. He was pretty sure that Colter had killed him sometime during the night.

But, like Danny, he was asking himself that same question.

Why?

CHAPTER

4

THE SKY WAS TRYING TO MAKE UP ITS MIND ALONG the eastern horizon. The sun fought to gain a foothold on the thick clouds that drifted and changed color from pale yellow to amber to gray. But Jed knew the sun would eventually have its way as it rose higher in the morning sky and the clouds began to break up and drift ever northward and eastward.

The cattle were strung out for most of a mile, but holding to the trail, bunched close by Colter and Jed. Colter was keeping the column to a width of 150 yards or so, while Jed and the remuda prodded them from the dusty rear.

He was still fuming over his brush with Colter earlier that morning. And he now had another worry, or at least a concern, over something else Silas had said to him when they were riding close together getting the last of the herd on its feet.

"One other thing, Brand," Colter had said. "You should not mention my name to the buyer. Just tell him yours."

"Why?"

"When I sent him a telegram from Waco I didn't know if I was coming up to Abilene right then. I had just had my drovers run off and leave me stranded, so I used your name in case I couldn't go."

"You sure as hell take a lot of liberties, Colter."

"It was the expedient thing to do at the time."

Expedient?

No, Jed was sure there was more to it than that. Colter had so many cards up his sleeve it was hard to tell if he had a real arm in there. The man was as slithery as a snake, and as hard to nail down as jelly.

What had bothered Jed from the beginning was that Colter was driving too many cattle with too few hands. He didn't have a chuck wagon or a cook. Colter hadn't wanted to hire Cardoza to wrangle the remuda; hadn't even wanted the Brands to bring extra horses.

Jed had no doubts that Colter was the kind of man

who would think nothing of riding a horse into the
ground if he got what he wanted out of it. It was no wonder all of his drovers from the Rio Grande Valley had
quit in Waco, or somewhere along the way. If that was,
indeed, what had happened. And no telling how many
head he had started out with. Cattle drives in those days
gathered thousands of head and the drovers had to fight
farmers and landowners in Missouri whose domestic
cattle were dying from the ticks brought in by the Texas
longhorns. They called the disease Texas Fever or Spanish Fever without knowing it was the ticks causing it.
Later, when they found out, they banned all longhorns
from entering the state and the farmers formed vigi-
lance committees and were waiting at county lines to
drive the Texans back at every opportunity. So, the cattle ranchers in Texas started driving their herds along
the borders up into Kansas and then even Kansas
wouldn't let any longhorns in until after the war.

Colter, by driving just a few head at a time, or so he
said, could avoid a lot of trouble from Kansas settlers.
And he was getting a pretty fair price per head, but
there was something suspicious about a man driving
only a few hundred cattle that far. A man would have to
make a lot of trips to make enough money to make the
venture pay.

If they hadn't needed the money, he and Dan would
never have signed on with a man like Colter. But Jed's
mother, Ellen, was in poor health. He had seen gray

come into her hair twenty years before her time. Their father had left them when both boys were in their teens. Jed and Dan had both had to work to help support their mother through the lean times of the war and afterward. She worked, too, but it sapped her youth and vitality. She scrubbed and ironed clothing, did sewing and needlework. The pay for each of them was low and they barely scraped by as it was, so Colter's offer of fifty dollars a month and food was a boon to the family, or so their mother thought. Dan, as well. Both of them had closed their ears to Jed's arguments against signing on with Colter, and reluctantly, Jed had relented and gone on the drive. But it had been a fight with Colter all the way.

The herd moved slowly, grazing as it ambled north toward Abilene. Some of the cattle were lowing and grumbling when they had to leave a patch of grass as those behind kept pushing forward. It was a slow process, and sometimes Colter had to let the herd fan out so that all the longhorns could eat.

Shortly after the last of the herd got to its feet and joined the column, Jed looked up. Something had caught his eye. A buzzard flapped lazily over a place some five hundred yards from him, then floated on invisible currents of air, scribing slow circles in the sky. As he watched, he saw other buzzards flying toward that same region, and then he saw the first buzzard spiral down to earth. As it landed, another buzzard leaped into the air, flapping its wings hard before settling down again.

More and more buzzards came from different directions until they looked like leaves in a windstorm, floating in circles above the spot where others on the ground were feeding on something. Something that was dead, or dying.

"Ho, Colter," Jed called, pointing to the sky.

"I see 'em. Turkey buzzards."

"Hang on to this rope while I go see what's out there, will you?"

"Brand, we haven't got time for you to check out what every buzzard's having for breakfast."

Jed rode up and handed the rope to Colter. Colter took it, but his frown said that he didn't like it.

"I'll be right back," Brand said, and turned Jubal toward the place where the buzzards were congregating.

Colter led the horses to the rear of the herd and watched for straying cattle. But he also watched where Jed was riding, and, when he was sure no one was looking, he reached over and grabbed the stock of his rifle jutting out of its boot. He slid the rifle up and eased it back down into its sheath to make sure it could come free easily in case he needed it. As Jed rode over the horizon, the earth seemed to swallow him up, leaving only the crown of his hat showing from where Colter sat his horse.

Jed saw the cluster of buzzards hopping around

something dark on the ground. They were fighting among themselves, jabbing at each other with their beaks, their wings flapping in protest and to escape injury. Some stood nearby the object, watching, waiting, while others descended on silent pinions from the sky to join the feeding frenzy.

The sun cleared the eastern clouds and blazed hot and bright on the dark shape lying on the sparse grasses trying to gain a foothold on a patch of ground that had been washed away by flash floods too many times to count.

As Jed rode up, the buzzards, looking like a gathering of ungainly undertakers, hopped off and took flight, their wings beating sounds out of the air that sounded like a woman whacking rugs on a line with a flat straw broom.

The buzzards had picked out the eyes, and now there were only two vacant sockets staring up at Jed, sightless and black as coal. Julio's throat was wide open, gaping, the blood dried to a dark brown. His mouth was open as if he had tried to scream in that last moment before his voice was cut out of him with one swift slash of a knife blade as sharp as a surgeon's scalpel.

Jed dismounted and turned Julio over. He had seen the drag marks and the back of Cardoza's body confirmed that he had been dragged by his feet to this spot and left for the vultures.

He rolled Julio's body back over and left it as he had

found it. A sickness roiled in Jed's stomach as he looked at the dead face turning ochre in the splash of sunlight, turning to dried leather as the fluids inside his skin evaporated in the boiling heat.

"Sorry, Julio. Rest in peace, amigo."

Jed's voice was alien to him in that grim moment when mortality rushed up to him like a fist in the gut. The lifeless body seemed so small and pathetic, like some rag doll tossed from a passing wagon, a scarecrow stuffed with straw and left in a field.

"I wish I could bury you, Julio," Jed muttered, feeling helpless against the wall of desolation that rose up between him and the dead man. *"Vaya con Dios."*

That was the only prayer that Jed knew in Spanish and it was really a way of saying good-bye to a friend. Julio had not deserved to die and he did not deserve to lie out here waiting for the buzzards and the coyotes to pick his bones clean as if he had been nothing in life and was now nothing in death.

Jed got up slowly and mounted Jubal. He touched a finger to the brim of his hat in a gesture of final farewell and turned the horse to head back to the herd. He put the spurs to Jubal's flanks and rode up on Colter and the remuda at a gallop.

He took the rope from Colter and glanced at the knife jutting from its scabbard on Colter's belt. It showed no sign of being used or bloodied, but Jed had no doubt in his mind who had murdered Julio Cardoza.

"Find anything?" Colter asked, with an airy casualness.

"Naw," Jed said. "Just an old sick coyote that died of old age, I reckon."

"See? A waste of time."

"Yeah. I reckon."

"Keep pushing this herd. They don't need to feed all morning. I want to get to Abilene."

"OK, Boss," Jed said, tightly. He couldn't look into Colter's eyes, because he knew if he did, that hate inside him would explode and he'd do something he might regret for the rest of his life. An eye for an eye. A life for a life. But now was not the time and this was not the place. He had no proof, but his hunch was so strong it was like something true etched in stone.

Colter rode off to the right flank of the herd. It would be so easy for Jed to jerk his rifle from its sheath, lever a cartridge into the firing chamber and put a bullet right between Colter's shoulder blades. For a fleeting moment, Jed considered doing just that. But he knew he was not a backshooter and more than that, he wanted to see the truth of the murder in Colter's eyes and make him squirm before dying at the end of a rope, or under the slice of a blade, or from a lead bullet burning through his flesh.

"One day, you sonofabitch," Jed said under his breath, and he breathed deep to clear his mind of the hate and the desire for vengeance.

And he thought of dead Julio back there lying faceup

in the washed-out place with the sparse grasses. He closed in on the rear of the herd with the remuda and barked at the lumbering cattle, waving his hat to get them to move faster. He wanted to get to Abilene, too. He wanted very much to talk to the sheriff about the murder of a poor, innocent Mexican boy.

CHAPTER

5

J ED NOW CARRIED A SECRET, AND THE SECRET WEIGHED heavy in his heart as the herd streamed into the Great Western Stockyard pens in Abilene. Dan and Colter had guided the lead cattle through the gates, then Colter had left. Jed was amazed at the size of the stockyards. The three hundred head did not come close to filling the big corral. Wranglers appeared and helped to keep the herd moving until the last of the longhorns was inside. One of the men closed the gate.

"When's the rest of 'em comin' in?" he asked.

"That's all there is," Dan told him.

"Where you from?" asked the young man.

"Waco."

"Pretty small herd to drive all that way. Want us to tally 'em?"

"No. Let the buyer make the count. As for the size of the herd, we go with what we've got," Dan said.

"These for auction?" one of the other men asked.

Jed shook his head. "Sold already. I think."

"Who you lookin' fer?"

"Malcolm Trent," Jed said, as he handed off the remuda to a youthful man who emerged from the livery, with a tangle of rope halters in his hands. "Grain 'em, will you?"

"Sure thing. Four bits a day per head if you board 'em. You want 'em combed and curried? That's another two bits for each horse."

"No. Not today. I'll come by and see what they need after I finish my business with Trent."

"Suit yourself, Mister," the boy said. He looked to be about sixteen or seventeen, and it looked like his hair hadn't seen a brush or a comb ever. His face was still sprinkled with freckles. "I'll take 'em over to the livery. You want me to take your horses, too?"

"Yeah. Dan, give him your horse." Jed swung down out of the saddle and handed the reins to the boy. "Sure you can handle all these at once?"

"Mister, you got a small herd and a small remuda. I've handled more'n this all at once."

Dan dismounted, too, and handed his reins to the young man. The two of them watched him lead all the horses to the livery barn. One of the wranglers walked over.

"I'll fetch Mr. Trent," he said. "He's over at the Drover's Cottage. Won't be long. Funny, he didn't say nothin' about no cattle comin' in."

"Maybe he wasn't expecting us this soon," Jed said.

The man walked away and Jed walked over to the pole fence, leaned against it. Dan came over and climbed up, sat on the top rail.

"Boy, am I glad to get these cattle in the pens," he said. "I'm plumb wore down to a nubbin."

"Dan, I got something to tell you, but you've got to keep it to yourself, hear?"

"Sure, Jed."

"Swear?"

"I swear. Ye gods, Jed, what is it?"

"I mean really swear. You can't breathe a word. Or even act like you know what I'm about to tell you."

"Cross my heart, Jed, for chrissake."

Jed drew in a deep breath, let out it. His brown eyes darkened, then flashed as they widened. Dan swallowed, waiting.

"I've been riding with death for the past eight mile, Danny."

"Huh? What in hell're you talkin' about, Jedediah Brand?"

"Julio Cardoza. He's dead."

"Plumb dead?"

"Dead as a stump, Danny. Did you see all them buzzards in the sky when we set out?"

"I saw some buzzards. Didn't pay much attention to them. Ye gods, Jed, there's buzzards ever' damn where. It don't mean nothin'."

"Well, these buzzards had carrion to feed on. I rode over and took a look for myself. Found Julio lying there with his throat cut wide open. Deader'n hell."

Dan gasped. Then he shook his head.

"Don't be pullin' my leg, Jed. That ain't funny."

"Damn you, Danny, I'm serious. Colter killed him. Last night. I know it as sure as I know my own name. Nobody else could have done it. It was Colter. I told you there was something fishy about that jasper. He murdered poor Julio while we were asleep."

"Lord, Jed. You got to do something about it. I mean, we do, I reckon."

"I'm going to the sheriff here in Abilene as soon as Colter pays us. I just wanted you to know what I been carryin' around with me."

"Why? Why would Silas do a thing like that? Poor ol' Julio."

"I don't know. But I think if I'd have said anything

back there, he would have killed me without batting an eye."

Dan let out a low whistle. He started looking around as if expecting Colter to jump up out of nowhere and start shooting at them. His face drained of blood until it was as pasty as pie dough.

"Jed, we got to get away from that man Colter. He's plumb poison."

"We've got to see him one more time. To get our money."

"Do you trust him, Jed?"

"To pay us, you mean?"

"Yes."

"I don't see how he can get out of it. Trent's going to give me the money and then I'll give it to Colter."

"Why don't we just take our money out and leave his for him someplace."

"That's a thought. But we'll probably get paid with a bank draft."

"Oh shit."

"We'll go with Colter to the bank when he cashes it. Don't worry, Danny. We'll get our money."

"Ma's counting on it."

"I know."

Dan lifted his pistol from its holster on his belt. He thumbed the hammer back to half cock and spun the cylinder on his six-gun, a converted Remington New

Model Army in .44 caliber that had been converted from caplock to centerfire. He was plainly nervous, his face bathed in sweat, his hands trembling slightly.

"Danny, put that damned thing away," Jed told him.

"I just want to be sure it works, Jed."

"You won't need it. We're not going to brace Silas."

"No, maybe. But, he might brace us."

"Don't be a goose. He wouldn't try anything here. In public."

"God, I keep thinking about poor ol' Julio. He was just a damned kid."

"Don't think about it, Danny. I'm glad you didn't see him like that."

"I never saw a dead person before, not since Grandpa, and I was so little at the time I hardly remember it. And I never saw nobody killed. Murdered."

"Put the pistol away, Danny."

Danny spun the cylinder so that the cylinder was off center slightly and eased the hammer back down until it was snug. He slid the pistol back into its holster, but made sure it was loose. He hooked his thumbs into his cartridge-studded gun belt.

"I wonder if I should get my rifle," Dan said.

"Danny. Stop it."

"Well, Christ, Jed."

They waited for the buyer. Jed looked down the street at the town of Abilene. It was mostly log cabins from what he could see and there were not many people on the streets. It was warm and maybe everyone was staying inside, but it did not look like a thriving town from where he stood.

A sign caught Jed's attention. In large block letters it stated: NO GUNS IN ABILENE.

"Dan, look," he said, pointing. "See that sign yonder?"

Dan looked in the direction his brother was pointing. He read the sign and shook his head.

"Wonder what that means, Jed?"

"It means there's law in Abilene." Jed grinned.

As they were staring at the sign, two men stepped off the boardwalk on Texas Street and walked toward them. Both men wore sidearms. Both men wore shiny stars on their vests. They crossed the railroad tracks and headed straight for the Brand brothers.

"Uh-oh," Dan said.

"We've done nothing wrong," Jed said. "Just let me do all the talking, Danny."

"Good afternoon," one of the men said. "I'm Marshal Tom Smith. You boys from Texas?"

"We are," Jed said.

"Are you planning to go into town?"

"I don't rightly know. We're waiting for Mr. Malcolm Trent to come and pay us for these cattle we just run in here."

"Well, if you cross those tracks yonder, you've got to leave your guns in my office. I'll give you a receipt and you'll get 'em back when you ride out."

"Where's your office, Marshal?"

"First building there on the other side of the tracks. You can't miss it."

"Tell him, Jed," Dan whispered, poking Jed in the side with his elbow.

"What's that?" Smith said.

"Aw, nothing, Marshal."

"Jed—"

"Shut up, Danny."

Smith, a flint-eyed man, lean as a whip, bored into Jed's eyes with his own.

"Something on your mind, cowboy?" Smith asked.

"No, not . . . I mean, if we come across the tracks, we'll drop off our pistols in your office."

"Your friend seems to have something he wants you to tell me. Are those cattle stolen, by any chance?"

"No, sir. He's my brother, Dan Brand. My name's Jed."

"Where you from, Jed?"

"Waco."

"Well, you're a long way from home. You keep your nose clean in Abilene and we'll get along."

"Yes sir."

Smith looked at some of the cattle through the fence. His deputy kept his eyes on the Brand brothers.

"Two Bar Eight, huh? Haven't seen that one up here before," Smith said. "Those all you brought?"

"Yes sir."

"Well, you boys get your business done and if you come into town, you stop by, hear?"

Jed nodded. Smith and his deputy turned on their heels and walked back across the railroad tracks.

Dan was having a fit.

"Damn it, Jed, that was your chance. You should have told that marshal about Colter."

"Danny, hold your horses, will you? Colter's not here and I've got nothing to back up my story. The minute I opened my mouth about a murder, that marshal would have put us both in the *juzgado*. I'm just not ready to go to the law yet."

"Well, when will you be?"

"After we get our pay and Colter's where that marshal can grab him."

"Damn, Jed. I know you're a lot smarter than me, but sometimes you seem awful dumb."

"Well, we won't have to wait long, maybe. Here comes a man walking toward us. I'll bet that's Malcolm Trent."

A well-dressed man with shiny boots walked toward them on Texas Street. He nodded to Smith and the deputy and they waved to him.

"One of you named Jed Brand?" the man said as he came up to the corral.

"I am."

"Let's go into the sale barn, then, and do our business."

"Are you Mr. Trent?"

The man shook his head. He was dressed like a banker and his short-brimmed hat looked newly blocked and was unsoiled. He sported a small brisk mustache and lamb-chop sideburns. He wore a vest under his suit coat from which a gold chain dangled.

"No, I'm his agent, Rufus Whitby."

"Where's Mr. Trent?" Jed asked, his tone laced with suspicion.

"He's busy, Mr. Brand. Shall we? It'll be a little cooler in the barn, away from the hot sun."

Whitby pointed at the barn and then started walking toward it. As he turned, Jed noticed something else the man was wearing, tucked into his lower vest pocket.

Both Brand boys looked at each other. Dan shrugged.

When Whitby was far enough away, Jed turned to Dan and whispered in his ear.

"Watch him, Danny. In a 'No Gun' town, he's packin' a derringer."

Dan swore under his breath.

Jed loosened his pistol in his holster. Just in case.

CHAPTER

6

THERE WAS A SMALL, SPARSELY FURNISHED OFFICE inside the large barn. Whitby seemed right at home there. He opened the door and ushered the brothers inside, motioned for them to take chairs and sit.

"Did you boys meet Bear River yet?" Whitby asked as he sat down behind the desk. He reached inside his coat and pulled out a fat envelope.

"Who's Bear River?" Jed asked.

"Oh, I beg your pardon. Marshal Smith. That's what

they call him. He has quite a history, especially here in Abilene. I take it you've never been here before."

"No, we haven't," Jed said.

"We'll be a few minutes. I have a man outside counting the cattle you drove in here today. Meanwhile, here are some documents to look over."

Whitby took two sheets of paper from the envelope and laid them on the table. One was a bill of sale, the other was a receipt for cash, with the amounts left blank.

"When we get the count, I can fill in the documents, but you should read them first."

Jed picked up one sheet of paper and began reading it. Dan did the same with the other document.

"Abilene has quite a history," Whitby said. "When it was platted that creek you might have seen on the way here was called Armistead. Then, when the war broke out, it was changed to Mud Creek because Mr. Armistead had joined the Confederate Army.

"The name 'Abilene' comes right out of the Bible, the New Testament, in fact. It means 'City of the Plains.' Wasn't much of a city, though. For some time it was just a bunch of huts, maybe half a dozen. Then Joe McCoy changed all that when he built all this, calling it 'The Great Western Stockyards.' Yes sir, Joe had a vision, a vision of a great cattle depot where you Texans could drive your herds to a safe place right on the railroad."

Dan and Jed exchanged papers and read them as

Whitby continued bragging about Abilene and McCoy's stockyards.

"That was back in sixty-seven. We built the Drover's Cottage where the cattlemen from Texas and the cattle buyers from the east could meet, eat, drink, and talk business. The following year, the town swelled and in came the pimps, the prostitutes, the gamblers, the saloons. Abilene was a wild cowtown, I tell you. Those look all right to you?"

"Yes," Jed said. "We'll sign when the numbers are all filled in."

"Be only a few minutes. My boys are good at tallying cattle and you don't have that many. Cigar?"

Whitby reached into his upper vest pocket and pulled out three cheroots. He offered two of them to Dan and Jed. They shook their heads.

Whitby got a matchbox out of the desk drawer and lit his cheroot. He put the dead match into a clay ashtray on top of the desk. He inhaled and spooled out a long plume of blue smoke. He leaned back in his chair.

There was a knock on the office door.

"Come in," Whitby said.

One of the young men Jed had seen earlier, who had helped them with their cattle, entered the room. He held a piece of paper and the stub of a pencil in his hand.

"Yes, Vernon," Whitby said. "What've you got?"

"Me'n Randy counted three hundred and four head of Two Bar Eight cattle."

"Sure?"

"I'm sure, Mr. Whitby." He handed the tally sheet to Whitby, who glanced at it and then nodded.

"Thanks, Vernon. You may go."

"There's a couple of marshals out there lookin' over the herd, Mr. Whitby. I thought you'd want to know."

"Smith?"

"No, sir, ain't Bear River Smith. These aren't Abilene marshals. They're U.S. marshals. It's Cal Garner and Leon Simms. Cal's got him a magnifying glass. Looks like they're checkin' those Two Bar Eight brands."

"No matter," Whitby said. "Mr. Trent has the authority to buy these cattle. They're being shipped east this afternoon. You and Dale get ready. There's a big herd due in this afternoon. About three thousand head coming in from Fort Worth."

"Yes sir." Vernon left the room but didn't close the door.

Whitby filled out the documents, then counted out the money in the envelope. He pushed the documents across the desk at Jed.

"If you'll sign these, I'll pay you for the cattle, Mr. Brand." Whitby stacked the bills up in front of him.

"Those cattle," Jed said. "We saw the bill of sale in Waco. They're legal."

"I'm sure they are," Whitby said. "As soon as you sign, the money's yours."

Jed signed the papers. Whitby looked at the signatures, then pushed the stack of money toward Jed. "Count it if you like."

"I will, sir."

Jed counted the money as Dan looked on anxiously. When he was finished, he nodded. "The money's right, Mr. Whitby."

"Fine. That concludes our business, then."

He folded up the documents, put them back in the envelope, which was considerably thinner, put it in his inside coat pocket and stood up. He ushered Dan and Jed out into the barn, then walked briskly outside, leaving the two men standing there.

"Now what?" Dan asked.

"I guess we wait here for Colter."

"What's all that about those brands on the cattle?"

"I don't know, Danny. But Whitby wasn't worried. So I'm not worried."

Someone came through the back door of the barn, his figure in shadow.

"Jed," Colter called. "Do you have my money?"

"Yes, and we want ours."

Colter walked up to them and held out his hand. "As soon as I count it, Brand."

Jed handed Colter all of the money. Dan licked his lips.

They heard footsteps outside the front of the barn.

Jed and Dan looked toward the open doors and saw two men striding toward them. Then they turned around to look at Colter.

"What the hell. . . ." Jed said.

"Let me handle this," Colter said.

"Those are U.S. marshals," Dan said. "I wonder what they want."

The two men wore U.S. marshal badges on their vests. And they both carried rifles.

"You men are under arrest," one of them said. "I'm United States Federal Marshal Calvin Garner and this is Leon Simms."

"I'll take that money," Simms said, walking toward Colter.

"What's the problem?" Colter asked.

"Those cattle are stolen," Garner said. "Someone took a running iron to the Two Bar Seven brand that was on them. As you know damned well."

Colter held out the money. As Simms was reaching for it, Colter dropped the money in a heap at his feet and drew his pistol. He was lightning fast. As the pistol cleared his holster, he thumbed back the hammer. Before Simms could react, Colter fired. The Colt belched flame and smoke, spewed out a lead ball that slammed into the marshal's heart. He dropped like a sack of meal, a hole in his back from the exit wound the size of a man's fist.

Marshal Garner went into a crouch and brought up his rifle, cocking it. Colter's pistol barked and Garner went into shock as the bullet smashed into his neck square in the Adam's apple. Blood spurted all over Dan, who turned toward Colter, clawing for his pistol.

Colter's pistol roared once again and Dan fell to his knees, a bullet through the middle of his forehead. He crumpled over as Colter stepped up and brought his pistol down with great force atop Jed's head, knocking him cold. Jed folded up into a heap.

Colter, with a calm coolness, reached down and picked up the money. He stuffed some in Jed's shirt, then removed Jed's pistol from its holster. He placed his own pistol in Jed's right hand, holstered Jed's pistol on his own gun belt. He walked out the back of the barn and outside to his waiting horse. Smoke wove lazy patterns inside the barn over the dead men, hanging over them like some wispy wraith in the dead silence.

Three men lay dead and another, with a cracked skull, sank deeper into darkness, blood seeping from a deep gash in his head, trickling onto the straw and earth of the barn, forming into a bright crimson pool.

CHAPTER

7

JED'S HEAD WAS A SEPARATE BEING.

It was a fire-breathing, snorting, throbbing muscle that occupied his mind, his body, his senses, even his fingertips. It was a demon he could not see, but which robbed him of his very identity while it boiled his thoughts to a scrambled mush of alphabet soup. He was sure, when his eyes opened, that he was in hell and was being tortured. He was almost sure of it when he saw the grizzled face of a devil not more than six inches away from him, moist red eyes glaring at him from a face that was covered with black-and-white wire all bunched up as if it had been squeezed into a ball.

"I wondered when you were going to wake up," a voice said. It seemed to be coming from that satanic face, a voice with a whiskey rasp and a deep bearish growl. "I have to put stitches in you, boy, but I need you awake to do it. If I give you the chloroform, you might not ever wake up."

"Huh?" Jed couldn't move. He felt paralyzed. There was pressure on his shoulders and someone was sitting on his legs, pinning him down to the iron cot with its lumpy, smelly mattress.

"You got quite a crack on your skull, young man. I can see bloody bone underneath the open wound. I'm Doc Bellum. James Bellum. That feller sitting on your legs is Don Kercheval, my assistant, and the man holding your arms down so that you don't knock my teeth out is Jeff Bryant, who's a swamper here in the jail."

"Jail?" Jed said, trying to refocus his eyes. Everything suddenly blurred when he moved his head.

"What's your name?" the doctor asked.

"Jed. Jed Brand."

"Well, Jed, Bear River found you in the barn with three dead men. The pistol in your hand had three bullets fired. Three empty cartridges in the cylinder of your pistol. Each of the three men had one bullet hole in them. Smith says you're going to be tried for murder."

"I never killed anyone."

"Um, well, you'll have to convince a judge and a jury of that. In the meantime, maybe you'd better start praying. There are other charges against you, too."

"Huh?"

"Cattle rustling, for one. That's a hanging offense, too. Brand altering. That carries a pretty stiff sentence. It looks as if they've got you hog-tied and branded for a host of criminal charges."

"I'm not guilty of anything. A man named Silas Colter killed those men in the barn. And one of them was my brother, Dan."

"Try to relax, Jed. I'm going to bathe that wound in alcohol and then start sewing up your head. You'll think I poured fire in it, but it's just to guard against sepsis. Now, hold still."

Jed looked up but the doctor slapped a wet towel over his eyes. Then he felt a hot stinging sensation on the top of his head. It felt as if fire had been poured into the wound, just as the doctor had said. Then he felt more pain as the doctor worked the needle and thread through his flesh, squeezing the wound together. Jed could feel all that and see it in his mind. His mother had sewn a cut on his arm when he was small and that's how she had done it. Jed winced and gritted his teeth. He did not move. The men holding him down pressed even harder once the doctor started sewing up the gash in his head.

Jed felt a last tug or two and then the doctor lifted the towel from over his eyes.

"Done?" Jed asked.

"Done." But the doctor smiled and poured more alcohol on the stitches. Again, the liquid burned like fire.

"Okay, Don, Jeff. You can let up now," the doctor said.

The men climbed off the bunk. Jed looked up at them. They both stared down at him.

"He don't look like no owlhooter," Bryant said.

"He's a Texan, ain't he?" Kercheval remarked. "Just like the rest of 'em. Full of piss and vinegar and to hell with the law."

"Now, now," Bellum said. "We mustn't judge young Jed Brand here until he's had his say in court. You'll get a fair trial, Jed, if that's any comfort."

"Not much."

Bellum laughed. He reached down and picked up a black leather satchel, packed away scissors, alcohol, needle, and waxed thread. He closed the valise and stood up.

"If it starts to itch, Jed, you leave it alone. It's healing. If it swells up and starts to suppurate, you tell the jailer to come and get me. That means you have an infection and that could be trouble."

"Likely he'll hang before that gets infected," Bryant said.

Doc Bellum shot the man a withering look.

"You mind what I say, Jed," Bellum said.

"Thanks, Doc." Jed tried to sit up, but the room spun around and he closed his eyes and sank back down on the bunk.

"Take it easy, Brand," Kercheval said. Then he called to the jailer. "Boggs, get us out of here."

Jed heard a door open, then footsteps. There was a jangle of keys, then a rattling of a key in a lock and the sound of the cell door opening. He saw the backs of the three men as they left, but not the faces, nor the face of the jailer. He closed his eyes and listened to the cell door clang shut. More clicks as the jailer turned the lock in the door. More footsteps going down the hall, then a door slamming. A loud noise as a bolt slammed into place. Then it was quiet.

His head throbbed and there was a series of piercing sharp pains where the doctor had sewn the stitches. It felt as if Bellum had stuck him with three or four needles and left the needles sticking out of his scalp.

Jed heard muffled voices coming from the outer room, which he took to be the jail office. He couldn't make out any of the words, nor recognize any of the men speaking. He kept his eyes closed and wished that the pain would go away so that he could think about his situation. He had no memory of being carried to the jail, so Colter had probably hit him pretty hard with something. He was sure it had been Colter who knocked him out. The bastard.

Jed tried to shut out the image of his brother Danny going down with a bullet in him. It seemed so unreal, but he knew it had happened. And he had been powerless to stop it. Everything had happened so fast. The U.S. marshals were a surprise, but Colter had been ready for them. All too ready. Dan had acted bravely, but it had cost him his life. And now he was being accused of killing not only the two U.S. marshals, but his own dear brother.

The voices in the jail office died away. It was quiet for a few moments as Jed lay there with his eyes closed, fighting back the pain in his head. Then he heard a rustling nearby, in his cell. His eyes fluttered open, but he did not move his head. He stared at the ceiling, the wall next to his bunk.

A moment later, he heard a hammering outside, the ping and ring of a nail being driven into wood. More voices, from outside the jail. Gruff voices that he could not identify.

"They ain't never hanged nobody in Abilene before," a voice said, so close it startled him. He had thought he was alone in the cell. Jed slowly turned his head and looked across the room. There was another bunk there and a man sat on it, looking straight at him.

"What?"

"They're building you a gallows, Mister. Right out there on Texas Street. They're going to stretch your neck."

The hammering grew louder, and he heard the slam and slap of lumber.

"I'm innocent," Jed said.

"I heard 'em when they brought you in here. They found money on you that had just come from the bank. They said it proved you sold stolen cattle and killed those U.S. marshals and that other feller, who was in on it with you."

"That was my brother."

"Yep. I heard that. That's why they say the judge ain't goin' to show you no mercy. You're going to hang, brother, and may God keep your soul."

Jed struggled to get up. He sat and let the room spin once again. Then he focused on the man across from him.

"Maybe they're building that gallows for you," Jed said.

"Nope. Not me. I got drunk in the Bull's Head Saloon, that's all. This is a new jail. Some of your Texicans burned the old one down. They don't take kindly to Texicans here in Abilene, Kansas."

"You don't look drunk."

"I ain't now. That was last night. I'll be gettin' out in about a hour. Should be a wild night tonight. A big herd come in a while ago and the Bull's Head will be plumb full. You might get yourself some more company before morning."

"Who are you?" Jed asked.

"Me? I'm Phil Coe and I ride with Ben Thompson. Maybe you've heard of me."

Jed's heart sank. He had heard of Phil Coe and Ben Thompson. Both were famous gunfighters. Everybody had heard of them.

What had he gotten himself into? What kind of town was Abilene?

For him, now, it was a town built in hell.

CHAPTER

8

JED REALIZED THAT HE HAD STEPPED INTO SOMETHING
that he was ill-prepared to handle. He looked down
at his bunk where his head had lain and saw the bloody
towels. It was no wonder he felt dizzy. There was a lot
of blood soaked into the towels.

Coe rolled a cigarette, offered the makings to Brand.
Jed shook his head.

"You lost some blood," Coe said.

Jed nodded.

"And I got kicked out of my own saloon."

"You own the Bull's Head?"

"Ben and I own it. But I got drunk and started fight-ing with a fellow Texican I don't like much. Ben wasn't there, so Bear River locked me up. If he hadn't, I might have killed that no-good jasper. He'll pay the fine, though, and I heard that the man I was fighting with lit a shuck for Texas."

"I heard Thompson was from Austin."

"That's right. He was born in England, though. Some little town called Knottingly."

"I know he was a Texas Ranger," Jed said.

"He and I fought in the Civil War together."

"I was too young."

"Well, you ain't too young to be hanged."

"I don't want to think about it. I didn't kill those men and I certainly didn't kill my own brother."

"Well, maybe the judge will believe you. He's honest enough. Fair, some say."

"Do you know a man named Silas Colter?" Jed asked.

Coe puffed on his cigarette, closed his eyes against the sting of fumes. His head was wreathed in a blue halo of smoke. He leaned back against the wall and waved some of the smoke away so that he could look at Jed.

"He's run some cattle up here a few times. Small herds, mostly. I talked to him in the Bull's Head a time or two, but he don't say much about himself. I'm a gam-bler and he sat in on a game once."

"What did you make of him?"

"Shady. Very shady. Fair poker player. Good at bluff-ing. Nervy, too. One of his drovers got likkered up one night and started ranting that Colter had cheated him. Colter heard him, walked up to the man and kneed him in the nuts. When the man doubled over, Colter took out his pistol and coldcocked him. Didn't nobody say anything, but Colter walked out and left the man. After that, nobody saw the drover again and some said Colter had taken care of him."

"You mean . . ."

"I mean Colter killed him. If the story was true. I took it to be true. You get so you can read a man's eyes. Colter has fish eyes. They don't talk none."

"Then how can you read his eyes?"

"A gunfighter stays alive by reading men's eyes. When you can't read 'em, you're reading 'em right. Colter's a killer. Ben said so, and I say so. You don't get eyes like Colter's less'n you've killed a man or two. I wouldn't play much poker with a man like that. And I didn't, after that first time."

"I wish I had you as a witness at my trial, Mr. Coe."

"I wouldn't make you a good witness, Brand. I've got too many notches on my gun."

Jed looked across the room, trying to read Coe's eyes. They were pale blue, like Colter's, and gave him the shivers. Cold, vacant eyes, just like Colter's. Unreadable, Jed thought.

As if reading his mind, Coe got up and walked over to Jed, looked him hard in the eyes.

"I know," he said. "I got the same eyes. Like Colter's. You got brown eyes. The best kind, kid. They can turn black and fill up with smoke and get cloudy. Brown eyes is the best."

"What do you mean?"

"If you want, if you learn how to do it, Brand, you can keep people guessing. Brown eyes can flash, can spark, can shoot fire. With those eyes, you can scare hell out of a man and maybe live a while longer. With eyes like mine, so pale, so cold, they're always boring into a man and they don't change. They look like death and that usually keeps men away."

"I never thought about eyes that much, Mr. Coe."

"Some people say the eyes are the windows into the soul, but I don't hold to that idea. I look for shadows and flickers and nerves behind the eyes. You got good eyes, Brand. They can hold on a man without blinking and a man has to look pretty hard to see in 'em. Me? My eyes tell a man he's going to die if he steps across the line. A man can read his own death in my eyes. That helps keep me alive, but it also tempts men with itchy trigger fingers. Those kind of men want to put my lamp out. And I got to draw faster than them, like Ben does, and put them down real quick."

"I can't help how my eyes look," Jed said.

"No? Well, if you live long enough you can, kid. You

keep them steady like you do and a man will think twice
before going up against you with a gun. That Colter, who
coldcocked you. He hit you from behind, didn't he?"

"Yes, he did."

"Well, that's because he didn't want to look in your
eyes. And maybe he didn't want you lookin' into his. If
you can read a man's eyes, you can see his intentions,
with cards, with a gun, with a woman."

"I guess I never thought about such, Mr. Coe."

"Don't know why I'm tellin' you all this, Brand.
You're not going to live long enough for it to do you any
good. Likely, before the week's out, you'll be droppin'
through that trapdoor they're buildin' out there and
your neck will snap like a twig."

Jed listened to the hammering. It was starting to
bother him. Coe walked away from him, stood before
the bars and looked through them at the empty cell on
the opposite side of the hallway. The hammers continued to pound and, underneath, he heard the sound of
sawing, and men talking to one another. He heard a dog
bark and a child laugh. They were building a gallows out
there. Just for him. And he was innocent.

Jed lifted his right hand and touched the base of his
neck, stroked it with his fingers as a man will stroke his
beard. He hated to think of dying like that, with a broken neck, his body dangling there, lifeless, but still kicking, like a chicken with its head cut off. Kicking long
after he was plumb dead.

Coe turned away from the bars and began to pace the cell. But Jed could tell that he was not nervous, nor restless. He appeared to be mulling something over in his mind. It was that kind of pacing.

"Brand," Coe said, "do you know what *muerte* means?"

"It means death in Spanish."

"And what about *el destino.*"

"Destiny, I think."

"Yeah, destiny. I'll be out of here in a few minutes, when Ben comes to get me, but I been thinkin' about your situation. You might get out of this, after all."

"Why do you say that?"

"Destiny. Maybe you're not supposed to die just yet. I got a feelin' about you. A hunch, maybe. And I've learned to play hunches. As a gambler, it can sometimes mean the difference between winning and losing."

"What is destiny, anyway? Like your life is already mapped out and you can't change it?"

"Maybe. If your destiny is to live, you won't die. I mean die before your time. If you got a destiny that says you're going to live to be an old man, then maybe nothin' can change that."

"But we don't any of us know what our destiny is, Mr. Coe."

Coe nodded in agreement.

"No, we don't. But I think we get an inkling every now and then. Your brother was murdered, and you want revenge. Or justice. It may be that destiny will play a hand in this. You might get out of that rope party so you can go after this Colter and kill him or bring him in to hang in your place. Something to think about, anyways."

"I hope you're right, Mr. Coe."

"One more thing and then I'll shut up. That *muerte*. The Mexicans say you sit with death. You ride with death. All your livelong days. They don't look at death as something to be feared, but more like a gift. A chance to learn, the way they put it. I don't know about that, but I do know we live with death. It's in us and around us. So if you live, if you beat the hangman on this business, you keep that in mind. Live with death. Don't run away from it. Because as sure as I'm standin' here, if you run, it'll catch you."

"I'll keep it in mind, Mr. Coe."

A few minutes later, they heard the latch clatter on the door and two men walked down toward their cell. One was the jailer, the other a sturdy bearded man, muscular and bulky, with a pistol on his belt.

"Ben," Coe said. "About time."

"I ought to leave you in here, Phil, you sonofabitch," Thompson said. "But the place is going to fill up tonight. Big herd comin' in now."

The jailer opened the cell door.

"Ben, this is Jed Brand. They're buildin' that gallows out there for him."

Thompson looked at Jed, nodded.

"*Suerte,* kid," Thompson said. "Luck to you."

"Thank you, Mr. Thompson."

"You 'member what I said, Brand. Death is sittin' right next to you on that bunk."

Thompson took off his hat and slapped Coe with it. Coe ducked and walked out of the cell, a grin on his face. Thompson put his hat back on and looked at Jed, touched the brim of his hat.

"Phil's right, you know. Be seein' you, Brand."

After they left, it was quiet. Jed wondered what Ben Thompson had meant when he said that he'd be seeing him.

Did he mean later, at the Bull's Head or later, in hell?

CHAPTER

9

THE HAMMERING AND SAWING WENT ON UNTIL LATE that night, and then it stopped. The voices faded away and moonlight filtered through the window of Jed's cell. That was when the loneliness and the melancholy struck him, plunging him into a hollow cavern of despair. He missed Dan. He missed his mother, Ellen. He wondered if his father was still alive, and if he was, where he was. He had never felt so alone. He almost hoped the marshals would bring in some of the drunken Texans who were carousing at the Bull's Head Saloon.

He could hear the muffled sounds of laughter float-ing on the night air, laced with the tinkling notes of a piano and the occasional rippling twang of a banjo and the high-pitched strains of a fiddle. If all had gone well, he and Dan might have been down there at the saloon, having a drink, listening to the music, talking with the other Texans about home.

Finally, Jed drifted off to sleep. The pain in his head had subsided and was now only a dull and distant throb that seemed timed to his heartbeat. The hard cot was a welcome bed after so many nights spent sleeping on the ground under the stars. He slept and did not awaken until the cell began to take shape in the early light of a slow dawn when a lone rooster crowed somewhere beyond the fog of sleep.

A jailer named Hoyt served Jed beans, beefsteak, and strong coffee for breakfast. When Jed tried to talk to him, Hoyt said he didn't know anything about his case and that he was going home when he was relieved in a few minutes. No one came to carry away Jed's empty plate for an hour after he had eaten. Then another man came for his dirty dishes and this man was uncommu-nicative as well.

Jed was beginning to feel that the lawmen had for-gotten about him and were just going to let him rot in that jail cell. All kinds of crazy thoughts bubbled up in his mind and he knew they all led down dead-end streets. There was nothing fruitful about speculating on his fate. He would just have to wait and see what happened.

Later in the morning, he heard a commotion out in the jail office. Loud voices. Then the door opened and two men approached Jed's cell. He recognized one as Whitby. The other man was taller and wore ordinary clothes such as what a cowman would wear. No fancy belt, no brocaded vest, no silk shirt, no fancy pants. His lumpy face was laced with spidery red veins around his nose, the sure sign of a drinking man. He carried himself well, Jed thought. The two men stood there for a moment. Then the jailer, who was named Anderson, came up, rattling keys on a large ring. He opened Jed's cell door.

"You can both go in," Anderson said. "I'll have to lock the door. Just holler when you want out."

"Thank you, Steve," Whitby said.

The two men entered the cell. The jailer locked the door and returned to the front office.

Jed sat there, wondering what Whitby and the other man wanted.

"Mr. Brand, this is Malcolm Trent," Whitby said.

Trent extended his hand. Jed shook it. There was strength in Trent's grip, maybe a sign of self-confidence, Jed thought. Trent didn't overdo it, but the handshake was vigorous. But as Jed looked into Trent's eyes, he saw that he was looking at an old man. There were puckers around Trent's mouth, lines in his face beyond the red veins. And there were saltings of gray in his hair. And, too, there was a sadness in his eyes, eyes that were wet as if he had been shaving raw onions. The pouches under his eyes added to the look of sadness on Trent's face. But Jed sensed that there was iron in the man, a determination that kept him not only alive, but vital. As if he were on a mission of some sort and would not die before he accomplished it.

"You're in quite a fix, Mr. Brand," Trent said. "May I call you Jed?" His voice was soft and deep, as if it were weighted with much thought.

"That's all right. I'm innocent, Mr. Trent. Silas Colter killed those two marshals and my brother."

"I know that, Jed. I'm here to help."

"How do you know I'm innocent?"

"Rufus here told me he found out who the real seller of those cattle I bought from you was. Silas Colter. I've had dealings with Colter before. Had I known it was his herd, I never would have dealt with him. He used your name on the telegram he sent."

"That doesn't prove my innocence."

"No, and it really doesn't matter if you're innocent or not. The town, this dirty, mean, drunken little town, has already convicted you, Jed. Two U.S. marshals are dead and someone must pay."

Trent walked over to the other bunk and sat down. Jed could see the inner frailty of the man. He looked strong, but he heard Trent's knees creak as he sat down.

Unconsciously, perhaps, Trent began rubbing one knee as if to knead the soreness out. Whitby walked over and stood next to Trent as if on guard, ready to tend to Trent if he needed his assistance.

"That's not fair," Jed said.

Trent chuckled.

"No, it's not, Jed. But, you're paying for some of the sins of Texans who came here to Abilene before you. Rowdies, hell-raisers, ne'er-do-wells, ruffians. They shot up the town, burned down the jail, and raised hell with Abilene's citizens. Until Bear River was hired and came here, this was a wild and lawless town."

"If they hang me, it's still a lawless town, Mr. Trent."

"Call me Malcolm, Jed. And, you're right, of course. I talked to Marshal Smith about you over at the Drover's Cottage this morning before I came over here. Then, Rufus and I looked at the evidence they have on you."

Whitby cleared his throat as if he were warning Trent not to go too far.

"What evidence?" Jed asked.

"Evidence that will never come up in court, I'm afraid. Even Bear River admits that. But he is powerless in the harsh light of public opinion.

"Evidence that can clear me?"

"Possibly. A good lawyer could probably get you off anyplace but in Abilene. I could probably get you off. But that isn't going to happen. As I said, the town has convicted you. As far as the fine citizens of Abilene are concerned, you murdered three men in cold blood."

"Like hell I did," Jed snapped.

"I like your fire, Jed. I like your gumption. You've got sand. Grit. But it's not enough to get you out of this pickle barrel, I'm afraid."

"What's the evidence that will clear me?"

Again, Whitby cleared his throat. Trent ignored him.

"They found a pistol in your hand, Jed. There were three empty .44 caliber cartridges in them. That showed that three shots had been fired from that Colt. But your cartridge belt contains bullets in .45 caliber. You own a Colt, I presume."

"Yeah, I did. Colter took it. And it was a Colt .45."

"Smith knows that you didn't kill those men. He believes your story. And so do I."

"And so do I," Whitby said. "Knowing what I know now."

"Be that as it may," Trent said. "I want you to listen to me very carefully, Jed. I am going to arrange your escape from this jail. From the clutches of Abilene. Tonight. You will not stand trial here in this scurrilous town."

"But . . . I want to stand trial. I want to prove that I'm innocent."

Trent snorted and got up from the bunk. His knees creaked once again. He walked toward Jed and looked down at him with kindly eyes.

"You're not going to stand trial, Jed. Do you know what they've done?"

"No."

"Someone, I don't know who, has replaced all those .45 caliber cartridges in your gun belt with .44s. In short, you don't have a case."

"So, I am being framed."

"Like a picture," Trent said.

Jed rubbed his neck, thinking of the rope and the gallows.

"It's just not fair."

"You keep saying that. Maybe it's starting to sink in. Now, you may wonder why I am willing to help you escape."

"Yes, I am."

"I'll get to that in a minute. First, listen to me. Tonight, at midnight, the guard leaves the jail to make his rounds. Before he leaves, he will unlock your cell. The door to the office will be left unlocked. There will be a saddled horse, your horse, waiting for you at the stockyards, tied to the fence on the farthest side. Your Henry rifle will be in its scabbard. Your pistol, with .45 caliber cartridges, will be hanging from the saddle horn. There will be ammunition and food in your saddlebags. Your bedroll will be tied behind the cantle."

"How . . . ?"

Trent rubbed two fingers together. "Money," he said. "What is indelicately referred to as bribes. All for a good cause."

"And what's the good cause? To free me from a certain hanging?"

"That's part of it, Jed. But it's not a free ride out of town. I want you to do something for me."

"And what is that, Malcolm?"

"I want you to find Silas Colter. And, when you do, I want you to kill him."

Jed rocked backward on the bunk. He looked up into Trent's eyes and saw the coldness there, the determination. He saw, in their glittering depths, the look of a killer.

"There'll also be money in your saddlebags, Jed. Lots of money. I'm willing to pay you for killing Silas Colter."

"Why don't you do it yourself?" Jed asked.

"Because, Jed, I'm an old man, and I'm dying. Before I go, I want Colter rotting in his grave."

Jed felt a chill run through his heart. He was being hired to kill a man he would gladly kill for free. He felt a great weight settle on his shoulders. He had never killed a man before. He had never wanted to kill a man before. And now, if he took Trent's money, he would be obligated to do just that.

"An eye for an eye, Jed," Trent said.

Jed slumped over, his mind racing. If he did what Trent asked, he would be no different from Colter.

If he killed Colter, he, too, would be a killer.

CHAPTER

10

TRENT'S EYES WERE BORING INTO JED'S. THE EYES were full of hatred. Jed could almost feel it, almost touch it. He dropped his gaze and the feeling was still there. It filled the cell and it filled him.

"There's more to it, isn't there? You're not out anything. You got the cattle you paid for."

"That's right. And they're already on the train heading east. I'll make a tidy profit on the transaction."

Jed looked up again at Trent. The man's eyes had softened some, but they were still filled with the smoke of anger, the murky wisps of a hatred that had arisen from someplace deep inside Malcolm Trent.

"So why do you want Colter killed?" Jed asked.

"I wasn't going to tell you that, but maybe I should. First, though, I want you to be aware of why it's so important you get out of Abilene before you come up in front of the judge, two days hence. I knew those U.S. marshals, one of them quite well. Cal Garner."

"I'm sorry, Malcolm. I didn't know 'em at all."

"Cal's got a brother. He's older. He's a United States marshal, too. Smith sent a telegram to him in Kansas City, told him about the murder, named you as the killer."

"So, does he want revenge, too?"

"He's probably on the way out here now. By train, I imagine. He wants justice for his brother, Luke does, and he might not wait for the judge to hang you."

"This Luke would take the law into his own hands?"

"No, I think he'd turn in his badge first. He and Cal were as honest as the day is long. I just want you to know how serious your situation is."

"I know," Jed said. "Now, what's the real reason you want Colter dead?"

Trent walked a few paces away, his back to Jed. Then he turned and stood still. Several moments passed before he spoke.

"Colter used to work for me," Trent said. "Back in Joplin, Missouri. I trusted him. But the man's greed was too much for him. I ran a freight outfit, and we had a large shipment of money come through. For safekeeping, I had the money in the strongboxes stored in my house while we waited for a wagon to take it on up to Kansas City. Colter wanted that money and he went to my house while I was at the freight office. My wife and brother were there. He murdered them both. In cold blood."

Jed swallowed hard.

"He got the money and left for Texas. I moved up here to Abilene, knowing sooner or later, he'd show up. Colter always wanted to go to Texas and get into the cattle business. He knew I was here, though, and stayed out of my way. This is the closest I've been to him. That's why I want you to go after him."

"Where is he? Where do I look?" Jed asked.

"He's burned himself out in Texas. I have reliable information that he's working out of Lawrence, Kansas, now. That's where you'll find him."

"How do you know?"

"One of his men told us he had set up a freight business there. But it's only a front. The man's a killer and a thief. He looks for opportunity. He preys on people. Lawrence is not that big. Someone will know him. He might be using a different name, but you know him. You know what he looks like. I'm counting on you, Jed."

"I don't know. I've got to be home. My ma needs money. She's been poorly of late."

"Jed, you have to make up your own mind. You have to determine where your loyalties lie. Colter killed your brother. What are you going to tell your mother? That you let his killer go free?"

"I don't know, Malcolm. I'll have to think about this."

"Well, you don't have much time. You have to leave at midnight. It's your only chance to escape the hangman's noose."

"I'll do what I think is right," Jed said.

"Fair enough," Trent said. "Rufus, summon the jailer. Good luck, Jed Brand. I hope you make the right decision."

"I hope so, too, Mr. Trent. Uh, Malcolm."

The two men shook hands as Whitby called down the hall for the jailer. In a few minutes, Whitby and Trent were gone. Jed sat there, pondering all the information he'd learned from Trent. He wondered if he could trust him, after all. Since coming to Abilene, he had met with nothing but deception. Deception after deception, including the replacement of his .45 cartridges with .44s so that he would be blamed for killing his brother and the two marshals.

The cell across from Jed's began filling up later that morning as jailers carried or escorted men who were drunk or beat-up or both. None were brought to his cell and Jed supposed that was because of the bribes Trent had paid so that Jed could make his escape that night.

Jed didn't know any of the men. None of their faces

were familiar to him. They looked like ordinary boys who had drunk too much whiskey and gotten into fights. Most of them slept and those who stayed awake were too sick to talk to him.

Shortly before midnight, Jed heard the door to the office open. He heard footsteps heading his way. Then, a rattle of keys and he heard the tumblers in the lock on his cell turn. He couldn't see the jailer's face in the darkness, and he really didn't want to know who the man was making it possible for him to get out of jail.

Jed waited, listening to the sounds in the office. The jailer had left the door open a crack and he could see a thin slat of light streaming through it. There were footsteps and a shuffling of papers, clicks of something metallic. Then he heard what sounded like the front door opening, and then a loud slam as the door was closed.

Quietly, Jed stood up and walked to his cell door. He opened it and was glad that it didn't squeak. He tiptoed down the hallway, stood outside the office for a moment, listening to make sure that the room was empty.

He opened the door wider and peered inside the office.

No one was there.

Jed entered the office, which was lit by a single oil lamp. His shadow on the wall startled him, but he took a deep breath and went to the door leading out into the street. He opened it and listened for several seconds.

He heard footsteps some distance away. They were going away from him. He slipped outside into the night and hugged the wall of the jail, trying to get his bearings in the darkness. Down the street, he saw streaks of light striping the street and heard noises from the saloon.

He looked toward the stockyards, knowing where they were, but was unable to see them. He crept along the boardwalk, staying as close to the darkened jail as he could. He passed another building and then he was out in the open, walking toward the stockyards.

His heart was pounding as he crossed an open plain, and then he saw the railroad tracks glistening dully under starlight. The moon was behind a cloud as he crossed the tracks and, ducking to keep his profile low, walked rapidly toward the stock corrals.

He saw no one and kept on, his feet treading fast in a brisk walk along the fence line. He went clear to the end. Then he heard a soft whicker and his heart leaped with quickened beats.

He rounded the last corner of the fence and there was his horse as Trent had promised. He approached it warily, not wanting to alarm the animal. When he came up on it, he touched its muzzle and spoke softly to it in a reassuring tone.

"Good boy," he said.

He untied the reins and slipped them around the horse's neck, held them together with one hand as he lifted his gun belt from the saddlehorn. He strapped on his six-gun and then put a foot in the stirrup. He climbed up into the saddle. He saw his rifle jutting from its boot.

Jed felt behind him. The saddlebags bulged, and, as Trent had said it would be, his bedroll was tied in back of the cantle over the horse's rump.

"Let's go, boy," he said, and turned the horse away from the fence.

The cloud drifted away from the moon and bathed the land in soft silver as Jed guided his horse toward the road out of town.

Then he heard something that stopped his heart cold.

Loud voices, coming from town. Horses neighing and men shouting in loud whispers.

"Come on, let's go get him," someone said.

He recognized the voice as belonging to Bear River Smith, the town marshal.

Jed clapped his heels into his horse's flanks and took off at a gallop.

He knew what the sounds in town meant.

There was a posse forming. And they were coming after him.

Someone, he thought, had betrayed him.

And now, he must flee for his life.

Jed knew that the odds were that he wouldn't make it.

The moon sailed overhead as bright as a lamp. He stood out, he knew, like the proverbial sore thumb. But his horse was fast and sure-footed. However, he was riding over flat Kansas ground. There was no cover to be seen anywhere.

He might as well have been riding down Texas Street, smack-dab in the middle of Abilene.

He wondered if Smith was a tracker, or if he had trackers in his posse. If so, and that moon stayed high, he didn't stand a chance.

He could only run the horse so far before he would have to slow to a walk.

Now he rode with fear clutching at his throat, his stomach in knots, and all of Kansas stretching out ahead of him like a dark tabletop where he could be seen for miles under the glaring light of the summer moon.

CHAPTER

11

JED KNEW HE COULD NOT STAY ON THE ROAD, BUT HE already knew that he was heading east. He took his bearings by the stars to make sure. The pole star in the Big Dipper was plainly visible in the night sky. Just outside of town, he had passed a road sign pointing east. The sign read: Junction City.

As soon as he took his bearings, Jed turned Jubal away from the road at a right angle. He rode far enough so that he knew his silhouette had dropped below any horizon visible from the road. Then he turned eastward again, walking Jubal, staying quiet, listening. Less than an hour later, he heard horsemen on the road. Sounds carried far on the night air and he heard men's voices. He pulled Jubal to a halt and cupped a hand to his ear.

To his surprise, the riders halted, as well. They were probably trying to find his tracks, Jed thought.

"Hoyt, hold up," a voice called.

Jed recognized it as belonging to Bear River Smith.

"No use goin' on," another man said. "It's just too damned dark."

"Then, he got away," another said.

"Boggs, I ought to string you up in his place," Smith said.

"I told you what I done, didn't I?"

"Yeah. After you let the bastard escape."

"I figured he wouldn't get far," Boggs said.

"Let's turn back," Smith said. "No use wearing out good horses on a lost cause."

Jed heard the men arguing among themselves for a few more minutes.

"We'll go after him in the morning," Smith said. "Hoyt, do you think you can track him?"

"I can try."

"Shit," Smith said. "Hoyt, you get two men and ride to Junction City in the morning. See if you can pick up Brand's track."

"Will do," Hoyt drawled.

More arguing. Then Jed heard them turn their

horses and start back toward town. He tried counting the number of men who were after him, but from the sounds of the hooves, it was difficult. Five or six, probably. And Hoyt was the tracker. He would have to keep his eye out for him once he got to Junction City. He had no idea how far it was, but if his hunch was right, that's where Colter would be. In the morning, he would be able to track him, perhaps, unless too many people had used the road since Colter left.

Jed knew that he was a pretty fair tracker himself. His father had taught him and Dan how to hunt and track game, and they both had learned well. Before their father left so suddenly and mysteriously, they had done a lot of tracking under their father's tutelage.

Jed thought of those things now as he rode through a land of shifting shadows, the grasses glistening with moondust as far as he could see, a strange nightscape filled with the fragrance of wildflowers and the cloying scent of cattle dung drifting from the stockyards, with wisps of clouds floating under the stars like silent wraiths and the moon beaming down at him like some watchful eye as the constellations spun in their slow and silent mystery as the midnight hour drifted off into memory toward the distant dawn.

His father would catch turtles, mark each one with a dab of paint, and keep them under a box. In the mornings, before the boys were awake, his father would release the turtles. As the sun was coming up, he would awaken the boys and tell them to track the turtles through the dew. If the turtles they returned had no markings, their father would send them back out and they were not allowed any breakfast until the correct turtles had been captured.

He had shown Dan and Jed how the wind would drift sand into a horse's track, or a cow's, and what the rain could do to animal spoor. He made them track bugs and lizards and snakes on hot, dry days, and they learned to sneak up on quail and trail them from their dusting places on long, lazy, summer afternoons. Sometimes, their father would blindfold them and take them far from the ranch on windy days and then make them count to a thousand or more while he rode a zigzag course back home, and the boys would have to track him to return in time for their supper.

Jed remembered all those things now as he fought against sleepiness and fear. He drank from his canteen, grateful that Trent had thought of everything, and before dawn, he fished through his saddlebags until he found hardtack and jerky, and chewed on those hard, dry foods until his stomach stopped growling and the nightjars went silent. Once, a floating owl passed overhead on muffled pinions and he nearly jumped out of the saddle as it whiffled past, ghostly in the pewter glaze of the moonlight.

Over the years, Jed had gotten into the habit of reading tracks everywhere he went. All kinds of tracks. Tracks of horses, dogs, cats, goats, coyotes, jackrabbits, rattlesnakes, lizards, quail, dove, buzzards, mice, rats. He developed ways to distinguish one hoofprint of a horse from another, looking for nicks, marks, the way a horse walked, ran, trotted, galloped. In his mind, he measured the gait of a horse and noticed where the hooves landed at each speed. He could tell if a horse was lame or how much weight it was carrying, or whether it was sick or tired, just by its hoofprints.

Now, he thought of these things because he knew if he saw the track of Colter's horse, he would recognize it. He would be able to separate that particular track from all others as long as he could see the impression of a hoof on any kind of ground. He was counting on that ability to lead him to Colter.

"Who was this Hoyt?" Jed wondered. A jailer. A tracker. But now it was no longer a matter of going after Colter. Someone was coming after him. Hoyt and two other men. Killers? Maybe. Probably.

Jed's mind traced through all the possibilities of what might lie ahead if Hoyt and the other two deputies found him. Would he have to shoot it out with them? What if he had no choice? What if he ran and they shot him? In the back? What if he killed them? All three? Could he live with that? How many others would Smith or someone else send after him then? He wandered through a maze of the intellect, with questions popping up like armed ambushers and answers shot down like silhouettes at a carnival.

As Jed rode on, drifting parallel to the road, close enough at times to see its faint ribbon slashing through the tall prairie grasses, his problems seemed to mount until he wondered if he should even try to escape the law. And if he did manage to escape the law, should he just dig himself a hole, crawl into it and pull the hole in after him?

What would happen to his mother? What would she say when she heard one of her sons was dead, the other accused of murdering him? Or, what if she learned that one of her sons was dead and the other a wanted outlaw? She would die. She would die of grief and of shame. That's what would happen to his mother, the poor soul. And how could he live with that? Knowing he had been the cause of her death? And was he responsible for Dan's death, even though he had not killed him? He had asked Dan to go with him on the cattle drive. So, in a way, indirectly perhaps, he was responsible for Dan's death.

It seemed, at times, that Jubal was plodding through heavy quicksand and that Jed was struggling along with his horse. He felt the weight of all these things on his shoulders and, as his eastward journey continued, they got heavier and heavier. He started to fall asleep. His head dropped down to his chest and then Jubal would step on something and change gait, jarring him awake. At times, he didn't know where he was and thought he might be back in Texas. He knew, then, that he had not merely dozed, he had actually fallen asleep.

He stopped at one point and got off the horse and walked for a while, fighting to stay awake. He lost his bearings another time and his mind was so befuddled he could not bring himself to consult the stars. And when he did look up at the constellations, he couldn't make any sense of them. He couldn't isolate the Big Dipper or the Little Dipper, or Orion, or any of the others. He had to shake his head and pinch his cheeks, and pry up his eyelids to keep from falling off the horse dead asleep.

He wanted to sleep. He wanted to just lie down and close his eyes and rest, even if it meant giving up his life to a trio of trackers.

But Jed didn't do that. He kept going, on and on through the long night, into the chill of it that at least made him shiver and helped to keep him awake. At those times, he wanted to stop and build a fire and lie down next to it and just sleep and dream the good sweet dreams he had dreamt as a boy back in Texas.

Jubal was tiring, too. His gait slowed to a dull plod. But he, too, kept going on, like a tired old plow horse in harness. The horse never balked, never stopped on his own. And Jed drew courage from the gelding, touched his muscles as a man would touch a healing stone and drew strength from them.

After Jed had crossed through the dreamscape of night with all its terrors and doubts, he saw a thin streak of light on the horizon and when he looked up at the sky, the black had paled to a thin pale blue and the Milky

Way had vanished. Soon, all the stars winked out, leaving only Venus, the morning star, sparkling in the wan sky and then it, too, vanished. The eastern horizon opened up like a rent in a black sheet and the grasses took on definition and he saw the road and headed toward it, gaining a second wind, the haziness in his mind brightening some. And when the road lit up as the sun edged up over the rim of the world, Jed glanced down at the road and saw tracks. Horse tracks.

A few moments later, he saw the track he was looking for.

The track of Colter's horse.

As plain as day.

CHAPTER

12

COLTER'S HORSE HAD A HABIT OF SCUFFING HIS right front shoe when he walked slow. This left a furrow behind the print, a faint one, but one that Jed recognized. The left front shoe was worn slightly more on one side, and the right rear shoe left a deeper impression. The left rear shoe had a nick in it that was distinctive, since twigs and pebbles often got stuck in it, producing another distinctive track that Jed could read with ease.

It took Jed the better part of three days to reach Junction City, and by that time, Colter's tracks had been obliterated by cavalry patrols, farmers, and other travelers. He saw troopers from Fort Riley more than once, but they rode off in the distance and he never spoke to any of the soldiers. He rode into Junction City at night so that he would not attract attention. To himself, he said, "I'm already acting like a criminal, like a wanted man."

Before he got to his destination, Jed went through his saddlebags and found that Trent had left him four hundred dollars in cash, which surprised him. That was more than he and Dan would have earned from Colter on the drive. He tucked some of the money in his boots, kept a small amount of cash in his pocket. He also found that Trent had given him plenty of .44 caliber pistol ammunition and he spent some time getting used to the Colt that had once belonged to Colter.

He liked the feel of the weapon in his hand. The forty grains of powder behind the projectile made a lot of noise, but the pistol didn't kick as much as he thought it would. It had a blade front sight and no rear sight, so that it slipped in and out of the holster easily. He practiced drawing it and cocking it with his thumb. He found that he was both fast and accurate as he shot at dirt clods and stones, shattering them with every pull of the trigger. And it had a hair trigger on it, which took some getting used to, even though he could see why a man might want such a feature. He figured that Colter must have done some filing of the sear. Just a mere touch of the finger would release the hammer. For safety's sake, he kept only five cartridges in the cylinder and dropped the hammer on the empty chamber so that the gun would have little chance of going off accidentally.

He put Jubal up in one of the livery stables he found on a side street near the eastern edge of town. The sign on it read: Wilbur's Livery, Feed, Shoeing & Freight. It was a half a block from the railroad tracks and near the road to Topeka.

"Are you Wilbur?" Jed asked.

"Ayair, Wilbur Simpson," the stableman said. "Board?"

"For a few days. I want the horse shod, too."

"Grained?"

Jed nodded, as he stripped Jubal of his single-cinched saddle, his bedroll, rifle, and the saddlebags, which he piled in a heap next to an empty stall.

Simpson was a thin, wiry man who looked to be in his late thirties or early forties. He wore a battered felt hat that had never seen better days. His face was clean-shaven and he stood no more than five and a half feet in his low-heeled work boots that hadn't seen a shine in five years or more. His fingernails were black under the rims, his hands gnarled and bony from hard work.

Brand walked along the stalls, looking inside each one. Down at the end, on one side, he stopped, his heart pounding with excitement.

"This bay mare," Brand said. "I think I know the man who owns it."

"Her name's Rose, he told me," Simpson said, leading Jubal into a stall. He took off the bridle and hung it on a dowel driven into one of the posts outside. He closed the stall door and walked toward Brand.

"How long's Rose been here?" Jed asked.

"Oh, a good two days, I'd say."

"And the owner?"

"Traded the horse to me. Picked him another'n. A big gelding, sixteen hands high, with good bottom, black as the ace of spades, with a small blaze on its forehead. A five-year-old named Satan, yairup."

"Where did he go, this man?" Jed asked.

"Said he was a-goin' to Lawrence."

Jed's heart fell.

"When did he leave, Mr. Simpson?"

"Call me Wilbur. Or Wil, if you like. Left here early this mornin'."

"Too bad. I was hoping I might see him before he left."

"Oh, he'll be back. Said he would, uhyair. Gave me money to board a couple more horses he said would be ridin' in this week."

"Two more mèn are coming here?"

"Uhyairup, that's what the man said."

"Colter?"

"Don't know that name. Man who got Satan from me said his name was Brand. Dan Brand."

Jed cursed under his breath. The gall of Colter to use his brother's name.

"Did he tell you the names of the men coming in this week?"

"Yairup, he did."

"What were their names?" Jed asked, his impatience beginning to creep into his voice.

"Uh, well, sir, let's see. One of 'em's name was Ralph something. Morton. No, Norton, I believe. Yairup, that's it. Ralph Norton and the other'n he said was called Fred Burns. That'un's a easy name to remember."

"When did this Col—I mean, Brand, say he'd be back?"

"Didn't say. Long ride to Lawrence and back. I don't figure him back here for a week or two, maybe three. Dependin'."

"Thanks, ah, Wilbur. Will you let me know when those other men ride in? But don't tell them I asked. I want to surprise them."

"You know them, too?"

"Well, I've heard of them, from Dan Brand."

"Where will you be stayin', young feller?"

"I don't know. Can you recommend a place that's close? Quiet?"

Simpson laughed.

"With the army right close ain't no place that's real

quiet. But, they's a hotel right up the street from here where travelers like yourself make themselves to home while they're in Junction City. Yairup, a right nice place and they got a kitchen and a saloon. Pretty gals, if a man's got the itch."

"What's the name of this place?"

"Why, the Cherokee Hotel. I didn't get your name, young feller."

Jed had to think for a moment. Two names popped into his head and he blurted them out.

"Trent," he said. "Trent Whitby."

"Odd name. I'll surely let you know when them two come in. But if they stay at the Cherokee, you'll likely run into them afore I can get word to you. That all right?"

"Sure, Wilbur. Don't forget to shoe that gelding for me."

"I looked at his shoes, Mr. Whitby. He's good for another month of hard ridin', at least."

"I don't want to have to worry about it. Just shoe him, will you please?"

"I'll do 'er," Simpson said.

Jed gave him some bills, enough to cover feed, boarding, and the shoeing.

"That enough?" Jed asked.

"More'n adequate, Mr. Whitby. It's a pleasure doin' business with you. You got a real fine horse there. I'll give him a good curry combing, so's he'll look real nice."

"Thanks."

Jed left his saddle and bridle in the tack room at the livery stables and carried his rifle and saddlebags with him. As he walked up the street, he heard a distant train whistle. The Cherokee Hotel was not hard to spot. It had a weathered-frame front and a large sign above the entrance. Lamplight flared orange through the windows, left distorted rectangles on the street outside. There were hitchrails in front of the boardwalk. Three horses were tied there, all with U.S. Army brands.

He checked in with the night clerk, signed the name Trent Whitby in the register and paid six dollars for three nights, which included breakfast, he was told. He heard voices coming from a room off the lobby. He glanced over and saw a sign above the door that said Saloon.

"Dining room's on the other side of the saloon," the clerk said. "Boss wants people to go through the bar in case they get thirsty."

The clerk laughed, and so did Jed.

"Room 105, upstairs. Looks out over the street, if that's all right? Everybody wants a back room and those are all taken. My name's George, if you need anything. There's a slop jar in the room, a water pitcher and a bowl. Bath's out back, four bits."

"Thanks," Jed said, taking the key from George. "I'll be down in a few minutes. Kitchen still open?"

"The dining room's open until midnight. You from Texas?"

"Uh, yes. Why do you ask?"

"Just thought so. You have that drawl that says Texas or down south. We don't get many Texans in here, but there was a man left this morning who said he'd been there. Name of Dan Brand."

"Let me know if he comes back anytime soon, will you, George?"

"Sure, Mr. Whitby. Likely he won't be back soon, but he left money to pay for rooms for two of his friends."

"Good. Maybe they're from Texas."

"Dunno. Could be."

Jed reached up and realized he didn't have a hat. He saluted George and climbed up the stairs to his room. He'd have to buy a hat. His was back in Abilene. He also wanted to find a telegraph office, or a place where they at least had a post rider who could carry a telegram and cash to Topeka, so that he could send some of his money to his mother. He would do all of that in the morning.

He set down his bedroll and saddlebags, took his rifle from its scabbard and leaned it on the wall next to the bed. He looked out the window, down into the street. The three army horses were still there. And there was one other, which hadn't been there before. The man must have ridden up while Jed was climbing the stairs to his room. It was a local horse, though. No saddlebags, no bedroll.

He was safe enough for the time being. But if Wilbur was right, two of Colter's henchmen would be in town soon. If he could befriend them, he might learn what Colter planned to do.

Whatever it was, Jed reasoned, he was sure that Colter had something in mind, or he wouldn't be expecting those men. And, whatever it was, Jed was also certain that it was probably illegal.

He washed the dust off his face and left the room, locking it behind him. He descended the stairs and walked into the saloon.

A man at the bar whom Jed did not recognize beckoned to him.

Jed walked over, blinking until his eyes became accustomed to the dim light. Three cavalrymen were shooting pool in a far corner of the room. They looked up at him briefly and went back to their game. They were drinking beer.

"Howdy, stranger, buy you a drink?" the man at the bar said. "I don't cotton to drinkin' alone."

"I don't know you."

"Nope, not yet. But a stranger is just someone you ain't met yet. And I aim to meet you if you'll belly up to the bar and let me buy you a drink. What's your pleasure?"

And that was when Jed Brand met Ethan Talbot, who would prove to be someone he needed to know at just that crucial time in his life.

CHAPTER

13

ETHAN TALBOT HAD THE KIND OF WEATHER-BEATEN face that showed he had been "rode hard and put up wet," as Jed's father used to say. He wasn't a young man, but he wasn't that old, either. He just looked as if he had lived a hard life. But he had a twinkle in his eye that told Jed that the past was over and he was making up for lost time.

"You got that far-off look in your eyes, friend," Talbot said, lifting his whiskey glass in a toast.

"I don't know what you mean."

"Down some of that and wash the dust out of your throat and tell me your name."

Jed was not used to whiskey, so he took a sip and felt it burn a raw path down his throat. But he liked the warm feeling the drink gave him and the way it took the tiredness out of his bones.

"Uh, my name is Whitby," Jed lied. "Trent Whitby."

"Like hell it is." Talbot smiled when he said it, but his words sent a chill of fear through him.

"It's what I use."

"Names don't mean much out here, I reckon, but you picked a real dilly."

"What do you mean?"

"I been to Abilene, and I know a man named Malcolm Trent. And he pards with a slick banker named Whitby. I figure you just rode in from Abilene, and you're lookin' over your shoulder, young'un."

"I thank you for the drink, Mr. Talbot. I'm hungry and I'm going to eat."

Jed started to leave, but Talbot grabbed his arm and held it in a tight grip.

"You haven't finished your drink yet and there ain't no need to run from me. I'm not going to bite you." Talbot paused. "Or turn you in."

"I think you've got me all wrong, Mr. . . . . ."

"Ethan. Call me Ethan. And I'm not wrong about people. Men, especially. You're runnin' from something, and if you keep that hunted look in your eyes, somebody's damned sure goin' to find you."

"What are you getting at, Mr. . . . Ethan?"

"You've got the look of an owlhooter about you. But, an owlhooter with no experience at it."

"That's the second time I've heard that expression," Jed said. "I heard it before in Abilene. I just don't know what it means."

"Owlhooter? It means someone like you. On the run from the law. Hiding out. Riding at night."

"Well, I'm not one of those."

"Maybe. But you got the look. I should know."

Jed took another sip of the whiskey. It went down smoother than the first swallow. More of his tiredness seemed to drift away.

"How do you know? Are you an owlhooter?"

Talbot laughed.

"I rode the owlhoot trail."

"Owlhoot trail? Is that a road, or what?"

"Son, you are a pilgrim, ain't ye?"

"I reckon so," Jed said, a sheepish look on his face.

"Likely, if you bucked the law, maybe back in Abilene, the marshal there will put out wanted flyers and maybe put up some posters on you, offering a reward. When that happens, the law will start closing in on you and you'll have to take to the owlhoot trail. No, it ain't no regular road, to answer your question, but it's a road all right, and it's dangerous and lonesome."

"I didn't do anything," Jed said. "I'm not an outlaw."

Talbot gestured to the bartender, holding up two fingers. Jed shook his head, but Talbot ignored him.

"I don't know what you done, feller, and I don't care. Maybe you're innocent. But your eyes tell me you're on the run and it ain't from no woman. I saw the way you stepped inside this saloon, the way your eyes combed over the room and the way you looked at them soldier boys over there. And at me. I've seen that haunted look on many a man's face and I wore it myself for a good long spell."

The bartender poured two more whiskies. Jed looked at the fresh glass and took another sip of his first one. Then he downed it in one gulp, which took his breath away. His eyes watered and one hand pressed hard on the edge of the bar as if he were holding on to the edge of a cliff. He felt his knees go rubbery for a moment, but he recovered. He wiped the tears away from his eyes by rubbing a sleeve across them.

"You ain't used to the whiskey yet, either. But you will be, by and by. A good drink can lift a man's spirits when he's feelin' low, and it can sharpen him if he don't take too much. It can also buy you a friend or two along the way, when you'll most need 'em."

"I don't plan to ride no owlhoot trail," Jed said stubbornly. "I have some business to take care of and then I'm going back home to Texas."

"Sometimes fate takes a hand in a man's life," Talbot said.

"I don't believe in fate. I think a man makes his own fate."

"Ah, a bright mind. That's good, my newfound friend. Then, what about destiny? Do you believe in that?"

"I don't know. I'm not sure what it is."

"Well, maybe fate is what befalls a man. Circumstances, you know. If you have gotten yourself into trouble, through no fault of your own, maybe that's what fate is."

Jed considered what Talbot had said. Maybe, he thought, there was something to fate, after all.

"If you put it that way. . . ." Jed said.

"And then there's destiny."

"What about it?"

"Maybe destiny is what a man is supposed to do in life. Maybe fate is what happens to a man on his way to fulfilling his destiny."

"I never thought about such things before. And I don't know if I want to think about them now. I'm tired and I'm hungry and this whiskey is something I'm not used to."

"I didn't think about fate neither. Nor destiny. Until I got caught up in both of 'em along the owlhoot trail."

"What happened?" Jed asked.

"I committed a crime, or so they said. I was just a

youngster, younger'n you are now." Talbot toyed with his whiskey glass, staring at it as if he were looking back into his own past. "A man I knew asked me to keep a strongbox for him. He didn't say what was in it, and I didn't ask because I trusted this man. Later, there was a knock on the door and my mother let in the sheriff and a deputy. They searched my room and found the strong-box. It was full of money. They asked me where I got it and I told them I had found it. I didn't want to tell them the truth. The strongbox had been stolen off a stage, at gunpoint, by this man I knew and he was hiding out. The sheriff said he was going to arrest me for stage rob-bery. I ran."

"You got away?"

"I did. I rode the owlhoot trail. And then I was caught."

"What happened?"

"I was sent to prison, at Fort Leavenworth. The money that was stolen was army payroll."

"But you were innocent, Mr. Talbot."

Talbot laughed.

"If a man runs, he's considered guilty by a jury and by the judge. I ran. I was hunted. Day and night. I stayed off the main roads. I slept in places where a dog wouldn't sleep. I lived like a criminal, so, in the eyes of the law, I was a criminal. I did my time and now I'm a free man. I paid my debt to society."

"What about the man who had given you the strongbox? What ever happened to him? If they caught him, he could have told the truth and you would have been found innocent."

Talbot looked Jed square in the eye.

"They never caught him. And he died without ever clearing me. My ma told me that he was sorry he had done that to me. He told her that just before he put a pistol to his head and blew his brains out."

"Who was he? Couldn't he have left a note that would have cleared your name?"

"He could have. But he didn't. People are surprising, you know. This man couldn't face either his fate or his destiny. He just quit. He quit on himself and he quit on me and he quit on my ma. He quit on life, period."

"I asked you who he was. This man who wronged you."

"The man was my father," Talbot said, and let out a long sigh.

Jed shook his head. There were tears in Talbot's eyes and they were shadowy with the pain of remembering. Talbot looked down then, and rubbed his eyes.

When Talbot looked up again, his eyes had cleared and they twinkled with a lyrical light as if he had just shaken off the ghosts of the past and was an entirely different man.

"To you, my friend," Talbot said, lifting his glass. "May fate be kind to you. May you fulfill your destiny."

Talbot drank, and Jed lifted his glass, finished off the

whiskey in it. It seemed to have no effect on him. But his stomach growled with hunger and he knew that another drink would befuddle him.

"Thank you, Mr. Talbot. I think. I'll keep in mind what you told me. Now, I've got to go and eat. Thank you for the drinks. And the advice."

Jed walked away from the bar on unsteady feet. He headed for the dining room. He looked at the cavalrymen as he passed, and they lifted their beer glasses to him and smiled.

Jed smiled back.

Just before he entered the dining room, he looked back toward the bar.

Talbot was gone.

Jed shook his head in disbelief. He wondered if he had dreamed it all. The whiskey was racing through his veins like wildfire and nothing seemed real.

The clatter of plates brought him back to reality. The smells inside the dining room assailed Jed's nostrils, stirring the juices in his stomach. He sniffed the aromas of sautéed onions, beefsteak, potatoes, beans, and boiled turnips. There were some other diners seated at tables. None of them raised their heads. He might as well have been invisible, he thought.

He sat down and picked up the slate that was in front of him. The slate listed the daily fare and the words blurred for a moment until Jed could bring his eyes to focus on the menu.

He felt like a fugitive at that moment. He did not feel safe. He wished Talbot had not left. He should have invited him to supper, so that they could talk some more.

Now Jed was alone. And he felt as if he were already on the owlhoot trail, a nameless, hunted man, wanted by the law for crimes he did not commit.

Just like Ethan Talbot.

CHAPTER
14

TWO DAYS LATER, JED WAS AWAKENED BY A KNOCK ON his door. He reached for his pistol while rubbing sleep from his eyes. He chided himself that such an act had become so automatic. But the day before he had seen Hoyt, Boggs, and another man riding by in another part of town. They had gone straight to the sheriff's office, carrying a sheaf of papers. Jed had let his beard grow and it was thickening on his face, feeling very much like a disguise.

He had bought a hat and new clothes, also, which

helped change his appearance. Jubal had been shod and when he took the gelding out for a ride, then back-tracked, he was satisfied that no tracker would know, just from looking, that it was the same horse he had rid-den out of Abilene.

He learned, from a waiter who took meals into the jailhouse, the full names of the deputy marshals from Abilene who were hunting him. He had found the small café on his second day in Junction City and made a point to go there for breakfast and strike up a conversation with the owner and his helper. The café was right across the street from the jail and the two men in the café talked about everything that went on inside the sheriff's office.

The café owner's name was Rudy Alberts and his cook and swamper went by the name of Willie Gorman. Willie was the one who told Jed that the marshal's deputies were hunting for someone named Jedediah Brand. He said the lead deputy was Lloyd Hoyt, and one of the men was named Perry Boggs and the other man was not a marshal, but a hired gun, a manhunter named Sorel Jellico. Jellico was a friend of Bear River Smith's, who had been a range detective, what some called a regulator.

"Jellico's a bad 'un," Willie told Jed. "Even the sheriff was scairt of him."

"That Jellico's been to Junction City before," Rudy said. "I saw him shoot down two men who tried to draw on him. He kilt 'em before their six-guns could clear their holsters. They was hardcases wanted for murder but Jellico never gave 'em no chance. Like a snake, he was. Them two hardcases were like mice, and he bit 'em. Whoever he's after, I pity 'em."

"Yeah," Willie said. "Jellico looks mean and he is mean."

Jed left the café and went back to the hotel, thinking he'd better pack up and leave town before Hoyt and the others found out where he was. He had hoped he could wait for Colter's return, but if Jellico was as quick on the trigger as Rudy Alberts said he was, Jed knew he was living on borrowed time in Junction City. He knew he didn't stand a chance against three armed men.

"Who's there?" he asked, then took several paces away from where he had been.

"It's me, Wilbur Simpson."

"You alone?"

"Yep. Got some news for you, Mr. Whitby."

Jed holstered his pistol, strode to the door and opened it, still wary. His right hand rested on the butt of his Colt.

"Come on in, Wilbur."

Simpson entered the room, closing the door behind him.

"Them two men you asked me to keep an eye out fer," he said. "Well, sir, they just come in not a hour ago.

You know, Ralph Norton and Fred Burns. Leastways, that's who they said they were."

"Take a chair, Wilbur," Brand said. "I want to hear all about it."

Simpson sat down at the small table. There were two chairs, but Jed remained standing.

"Ain't got much time. Livery's 'bout full up. Don't know why. Junction City's gettin' right crowded."

"You can say that again."

"What's 'at?"

"Never mind. Tell me about Burns and Norton. What are they riding? What did they say? Where are they staying?"

"Hold on now, Bud. I can only answer one question at a time."

Jed reached into his pocket and fished out a one-dollar bill. He sat down and shoved it across the table. Simpson picked it up, stuck it in his shirt pocket.

"Take your time," Brand said. "Just start at the beginning."

"They did not say much. They paid for two days' boarding of their horses. They said they would stay at the Junction Hotel. They rode good strong horses, shod no more than a few days ago, I'd say."

"They say anything about Colter?"

"Who is Colter?"

"The man who calls himself Dan Brand."

"They said they were expecting a man, but they did

not tell me his name. They said he would ask for them. Maybe tomorrow."

"They said 'tomorrow'?"

"Yes, they said they were expecting him tomorrow."

"Thanks, Wilbur."

"What will you do, Mr. Whitby?"

"Nothing, right now. Let's just keep this between ourselves, all right?"

Simpson got up from the table. Jed let him out and locked the door. He put away his saddlebags and stopped packing. He could not leave now. If Colter was coming in tomorrow, he had to be in town. When he sat down on the edge of his bed and thought about all of these events, he felt a quivering in his stomach. Was it fear or just nerves? Maybe both, he decided. He didn't know if he could kill a man, even in self-defense.

His thoughts roamed back to a time when his father was teaching him and Dan about shooting pistols. He was about twelve years old at the time and he remembered how thrilled he was that he was finally going to get to shoot his father's cap and ball. His father had two of them, both were Colts, but one was a .32 caliber, the other a .44. He and Dan started out on the .32. His father taught them how to clean the gun and load the cylinders with powder, ball, and bear grease. Then he showed them how to put the percussion caps on the nipples. He only loaded five of the cylinders, telling them that it was the safest way to carry a pistol. That way, they were less likely to shoot their feet off.

After he and Dan had shot at targets that their father had set up, and both had done pretty well, their father sat them down and spoke to them about the responsibilities that came with owning and carrying a pistol or rifle.

"I want you boys to listen real careful," their father had said that day. "What I got to tell you is real important. When you pack a gun, you got to put your temper away. Put it in another pocket."

"Why, Pa?" Danny had asked.

"Well, because you might get in an argument or a fight, and if you have a pistol on you, and the other man has one, too, the temptation to settle the fight with a gun is mighty powerful."

"What if a man draws his gun on me?" Jed had asked.

"If it comes to that, the argument has gone too far. I hope you will walk away and not try and settle it with a bullet."

"What if you can't walk away?" Danny had asked.

"Look, boys, sometimes you can't just walk away. But I want you to know that if you draw your pistol on a man, you have to use it, and use it quick. A gun is nothing but a tool, in the right hands, but there are bad men who use it as a weapon. And that is one of its purposes. But, to kill a man, that's something you have to live with the rest of your life. You have to think long and hard before you use that tool as a weapon."

"Pa," Jed had asked, "did you ever have to shoot a man?"

"Did you ever kill anybody?" Danny asked.

"You boys can't use me as an excuse. What I did or didn't do makes no difference. If it comes to the point where you might have to shoot a man, kill him, then you've got to go deep down inside yourself where your conscience lies and ask yourself if it's necessary. Or, in some cases, you might have to ask yourself if you want to live or die."

"Self-defense," Jed said.

"Yes, Jed. Don't never kill anything needlessly. Don't never shoot no man less'n he deserves it, and when you draw down on someone who's trying to kill you, you watch his eyes, not his hands. You see if you can read his intentions and then you take up the gun. And you'd better be prepared to take a man's life, and suffer the consequences."

"What are consequences?" Danny asked.

"What comes after, Danny. You got to live with what you done. If you take a man away from his family like that, his brothers or other kin might come after you. Or the law. There's a whole bunch of things can happen. Them are consequences."

Jed wondered what the consequences would be if he had to defend himself against those marshals, or Jellico? Would he then be guilty of murder, after all? Would killing any one of them mean that their kin would come after him, hunt him down for the rest of his days?

And, what about Colter? What if he faced Colter and came out the better man, killed him? Would that be murder, or self-defense?

What if he had to kill Colter, Burns, and Norton? All three?

Jed felt a tightening in his chest. The room seemed to grow smaller, closing him in, taking away his breath. What his father had told them, so long ago, was sound advice. He wondered if his father had killed anyone, and if, as he had said, there were consequences. What if that man's kin had come after his pa and that was why he disappeared? Was that why his father had run away from home, left his family?

Jed didn't know, but he thought that might be what had happened. His mother didn't know either, but he had heard whispers and he had listened to them talking in low voices late at night, and he thought maybe his father had said something about killing a man. But if his mother knew anything, she had never told him or Dan. If his father had a secret, his mother had kept it.

And now, he wondered if he would ever see his mother again.

Maybe he should just leave Junction City and go back home and leave Colter and his henchmen be. Maybe he should just run from the law and hope they would forget about him, let him live the rest of his life in peace.

But even as he thought these things, he knew that he

could not run. He could not let Colter get away with murder.

The room closed in on him, suffocating him, and he knew he had to get outside of it, talk to someone, put these dark thoughts out of his mind. For a while, at least.

One thing he knew, though, as he arose from the bed and started for the door.

He was going to kill at least one man. And maybe he would be killed as well.

He could almost hear his father's voice, loud and clear in his mind.

If you kill a man, you will have to suffer the consequences.

CHAPTER

15

J ED WALKED DOWN TO THE LOBBY, AND THE DESK CLERK looked up, saw him, then quickly glanced down, as if avoiding any further eye contact. Jed walked over.

"Something on your mind?" he asked.

"Uh, no sir, ah, nothing. I, uh, I just thought you looked familiar."

"I've been here three days. I should look familiar."

"Uh, I mean. Nothing, sir. You look like somebody else, I guess."

Jed knew the man was squirming. Something was

very wrong. The clerk was suspicious about something. He was about to question the man further when he heard someone hiss at him from the entrance to the saloon.

"Psst, come here, Trent."

Jed couldn't see who it was standing in the shadows, and he was not used to being called by that assumed name, so it took him several seconds before he realized who had hailed him.

Ethan Talbot stepped into the lobby, gesturing for Brand to come to him.

"Mister," Jed said to the desk clerk, "you'd better get out of the habit of staring at your guests. Some of 'em might take offense."

"Yes, sir. Sorry, sir."

The clerk was obviously flustered and Jed hoped he had quieted some of his suspicions. He didn't know what was behind it, but he knew he could not linger much longer in Junction City. Or, for that matter, stay at the Cherokee much longer.

He strode into the bar, blinking his eyes to adjust them to the darkness. Talbot was sitting at the bar, a drink and a piece of paper in front of him.

"Sit down, Pilgrim," Talbot said. "I've ordered you a whiskey. You're going to need it, I think."

Jed sat down, noticing that Talbot had put a hand over the piece of paper in front of him so that Jed couldn't see what was written on it.

"Why do I need whiskey?" Jed asked, as the bartender set a glass on the bartop and poured it nearly full.

Talbot waited until the bartender set the bottle down behind the bar and walked away. He went back to talking to two men at the other end of the bar.

"Take a look at this, Mr. Jed Brand." Talbot pushed the piece of paper toward Jed.

Jed's face registered surprise. His eyebrows arched and his eyes widened. Talbot had called him by his real name.

Jed picked up the piece of paper and stared at it. There was his name in bold black letters.

"Doesn't much resemble you, Jed," Talbot said. "Now that you're growin' a beard. But if someone was to take a piece of charcoal or a lead pencil, and . . ."

Jed stared at the drawing of his face. It did not look like him at all, he thought. But it did resemble a young man his age and the nose and eyes seemed to be set in the right places. The mouth was close, maybe a little thicker than his own.

"I'm a wanted man, Ethan."

Ethan grinned.

"Not too wanted just yet, young Jed. They're only offering two hunnert dollars for your hide."

Jed saw the large figures: $200.00. And, beneath it, the words, Dead or Alive.

"This is not good," Jed said. He turned the paper over and laid it back on the bartop upside down.

"These are all over town, Jed. Pretty soon, they'll be all over the territory and men will carry them to post offices and stage stops and mercantile stores far and wide. You'll be famous."

"I don't like the 'dead or alive' part."

"No. Did you see what your crimes were, the ones you're accused of? And that line about being armed and dangerous?"

Jed turned the flyer over and looked at it again. His face drained of color. He was wanted for the murder of two U.S. marshals and his own brother. And he was considered armed and dangerous. The bounty on his head was to be paid either at the marshal's office in Abilene or at any U.S. marshal's office upon proof of death or surrender of the fugitive.

"I didn't do these things, Ethan. I didn't kill any of these men. Certainly not my own brother."

"Better take some of that whiskey now, Jed. You're shakin' like a dog shittin' peach pits."

Jed looked at the glass of whiskey. It would not help the storm in his mind, he knew, but it might calm his jangling nerves. He reached for the glass as he put the flyer back down, again, turning it over so that the blank side was facing up. He drank half of the shot glass straight down, barely tasting it. The whiskey hit his stomach like a ball of liquid fire and he gulped in a breath until the flames went out and left only a warm spot in his belly. His hands steadied some.

Talbot held up his own glass, stared into its amber depths.

"Whiskey calms the raging waters," he said. "As long as you don't overdo it. You're going to need your wits, Jed, so I'm not buyin' you no more drinks."

"No. I've had enough when I finish this. Thanks. The whiskey helped. I've got a whole lot going on in my mind and this flyer really puts a great big old bug in the ointment."

"Maybe you better talk it out, while we have a chance," Talbot said. "Why don't you tell me what happened back in Abilene and what you plan to do?"

Jed told him the whole story about Colter and the murders of the two U.S. marshals and Dan. Then he told him about the posse and the men who were now in Junction City looking for him.

"Besides Boggs and Hoyt," Jed said, "they've got a hired gun on my track, a man named Jellico."

Talbot blew a low whistle through pursed lips.

"Jellico," he said.

"You know him?" Jed asked.

"I don't know the man, but I know his reputation. They must want you pretty bad to send a killer like Jellico after you."

Jed felt his face flush with a rush of blood and then his hands began to sweat. They felt clammy and cold.

"They're making a big mistake, Ethan. I'm innocent."

"But you can't prove it."

"No, I can't."

"Let me tell you something, Brand. Jellico is only going to read one part of that flyer there. The part that says 'dead.' He's never brought in a man alive yet. He's a cold-blooded sonofabitch. I think he enjoys putting a man's lamp out. You stay clear of him."

"I haven't told you the rest of it, Ethan. Colter's coming back to Junction City and two men are here now, waiting for him. Maybe you know them, too."

"What are their names?"

"One of them's named Norton, the other is Fred Burns. I don't know what they're up to with Colter, but they might get in the way when I brace Colter about the murder of my brother."

"How did you find out that Norton and Burns were in town?"

Jed told him about Wilbur Simpson's visit to his room that morning.

Talbot said nothing for several seconds. He seemed to be mulling something over in his mind. Jed waited, watching Talbot's face for any sign of what he might be thinking at that moment.

Finally, Talbot licked his lips and squinched his face up with a look of distaste.

"Jed, my lad, you're in a heap of trouble. No question about it. But I've got some advice for you, if you'll take it."

"Sure. I'm damned near desperate."

"Oh, you're plumb desperate, Jed Brand. If not, you soon will be. I declare, I've never seen nobody who's in so much trouble all at once."

"What's your advice?" Jed asked.

"Not much, I'm afraid. But, number one, if you ever plan to clear yourself of these murder charges against you, is that you've got to stay clear of the marshal's deputies from Abilene. You cannot afford to kill either one of them. You got that?"

"Yes. But how?"

"I don't know. Maybe they'll go back to Abilene or go on to Topeka or Lawrence. Hard tellin'. They might go back and leave Jellico on your trail to do the dirty work. Him, you can shoot, if you get the chance. Ever kill a man?"

Jed shook his head.

"Well, you may have to, Jed. Now, about Colter. If you're going to take him down, you'll have to do it when he's by himself, not with those two gunslingers waiting here for him."

"I ought to just go back home to Waco," Jed said.

"If you do, that's where they'll corner you," Talbot said. "You're in a box now, but you'll be in a cage back home. No, if you're going to get out of this, you're going to have to take the bit in your teeth. Colter seems to be the man you have to either capture or kill. If you capture him, maybe Smith can beat a confession out of him. If you kill him, you've solved only one of your problems, vengeance."

"I want Colter to pay for what he done."

"Well now, you're not just facing Colter. You've got his two friends, those hardcases, Burns and Norton. Three against one."

"And with Boggs, Norton, and Jellico, it's six against one."

Talbot shook his head. He lifted his glass to polish off his drink. Before he could bring it to his lips, a man's frame filled the doorway. Even in silhouette, Talbot could see his face, the clothes he was wearing, the pistol, low-slung, on his gun belt.

"Uh oh," Talbot whispered. "Don't turn around, but here comes trouble."

Jed froze.

"Brand, you step away from that bar with your hands up, or I'll blow you clear to kingdom come."

The man's voice boomed into the saloon.

Then there was a silence.

In the stillness, Jed could hear his heart beat, could feel his pulse hammering in his ear with all the insistence of a ticking clock. In that instant, his mind cleared of all doubt, all confusion. He knew he was standing on the edge of an abyss, a deep chasm, and at any moment, he knew he might plunge into the darkness that was death.

CHAPTER
16

JED SLOWLY TURNED HIS HEAD TO GLANCE AT THE doorway. Behind the silhouetted man standing there, blocking some of the light from the lobby, he saw the smirking desk clerk, holding a flyer in his hand.

There was Boggs, his arm dangling at his side, his hand a soft claw ready to snatch his pistol from its low-slung holster tied to his leg.

"Just raise your hands high, Brand," Boggs said, "and step down from that stool."

"Who are you talking to?" Talbot said, an almost amiable tone to his voice.

"Not you, bucko," Boggs said.

Jed raised his hands and stepped off the stool. He stood in front of Talbot, blocking Boggs's view of him.

"Me? You mean me?"

"You're Brand, ain't ye?"

"No, sir. My name's Whitby."

"In a pig's eye," Boggs said, then snaked his hand down to his pistol butt. His fingers slid around the grip. Jed's heart skipped a beat as he saw the speed of Boggs's hand.

Behind him, Jed heard a faint whisper, a slight scraping sound like metal sliding across leather. Then he heard a faint snick as if from the slow cocking of a pistol hammer. He felt something touch his left side and then he heard a deafening roar. Smoke and flame, sparks that stung him, flashed past him and he saw Boggs's pistol clear leather at the same time as a dark hole appeared in his chest. Dust flared from his shirt as the bullet spanked the cloth as it entered his body at over 3,000 feet per second.

Boggs's legs buckled and a look of surprise spread across his face. He squeezed the trigger of his pistol, a double-action Smith & Wesson .38. The pistol bucked and belched flame, spewing a lead bullet into the floor some ten feet in front of him. Then his gun hand went limp and his pistol clattered to the floor, uncocked, a useless chunk of blued metal with buckhorn grips.

Jed dropped his hands and he jerked his .44 from its holster and stepped to one side, went into a fighting crouch. Behind Boggs, the desk clerk brought his hand up to his mouth. His face went bone-white and his eyes rolled in their sockets, like marbles pointing to the ceiling. The clerk fell like a sack of spuds in a dead faint, his head striking the lobby carpet with a dull thud.

"Better get your belongings, Jed," Talbot said, "and light a shuck."

Jed walked up to Boggs, cocking his pistol. He looked down at the wounded man. Boggs's head was cockeyed on his shoulders, jammed to the floor where it had struck. Blood gushed from a walnut-size hole in his back where Talbot's lead bullet had torn through the flesh as it exited and sped on, spent to a wall in the lobby, where it chinked off plaster and paint and lodged there, its lethal force expended.

"He's dead," Talbot said. "Now get the hell out of here before this place is swarming with lawmen and gawkers. I'll cover you as best I can."

"What will you do?" Brand asked.

"Never mind about me, Jed. Go."

Jed strode out into the lobby, his pistol at the ready, looking left and right and out the front window. He waded through wisps of barrel smoke that hung in the fetid air of the hotel lobby like a gray pall. He walked over to the wall where Talbot's spent bullet was embedded. He took his knife from its sheath and dug out the mashed chunk of lead, stuck it in his pocket.

"What'd you do that, for?" Talbot asked from across the room where he stood next to Boggs's body.

"Just in case someone wants to check calibers, Ethan."

"You learned a lot, ain't you?"

"I learned that you can pin a murder on a man that way, by switching guns. Now they can't compare calibers from either your pistol or mine."

"You tryin' to protect me?"

"Maybe," Jed said, turning away from Talbot.

He took the steps up to his room three at a time. He eased the hammer down on his Colt and holstered it as he put the key into the lock and entered his room.

Quickly, Jed rammed his Henry rifle in its sheath, grabbed up his bedroll and saddlebags, and left the room, leaving the door ajar, the key still in it. He approached the stairs, listening for the sound of voices. He heard nothing, only the sound of his own labored breathing. He descended the stairs, his saddlebags slung over one shoulder, his bedroll and rifle in his left hand. He drew his pistol halfway down and cocked it.

Talbot was standing beside the front door, looking through the window out at the street. People were starting to gather on the opposite side, gawking and staring at the hotel.

"Hurry, Jed," Talbot said. "If you go to Lawrence, I'll meet you there in a week or so. Go to the Red Dog Saloon."

"Thanks, Ethan. I'm mighty—"

Talbot shoved Jed through the door, which he had opened with his foot. Jed ejected onto the street. The people across the way scattered when they saw the pistol in his hand, and one man ran fast down the middle of the street, heading for the sheriff's office, Jed surmised.

Wilbur Simpson was standing outside the livery when Jed ran up lugging his belongings. The stableman was staring past Jed, up the street, shading his eyes with both hands.

"Nobody's chasin' you yet, Brand," Simpson said, dropping his hands.

"You know my name?"

"There was a flyer on you when I got back. Not a good likeness, but I recognized you."

Jed was puffing from exertion, each breath burning holes in his lungs.

"Are you going to hold me up?"

"No sir," Simpson cackled. "I done saddled your horse. Here, gimme them saddlebags."

Jed handed him the saddlebags and both men entered the barn. Jubal was saddled, as Simpson had said, and was tied to a post near the back door. Simpson slung the saddlebags over the horse's rump, then grabbed the rifle and boot from Jed. Jed tied his bedroll on behind the cantle.

"I appreciate this, Wilbur," Jed panted. "What do I owe you?"

"You're paid up, I figure. If you get shot when you ride out of here, I'll put in a claim when they bury you."

Simpson was smiling.

"How much time do I have?"

"I didn't see nobody a-follerin' you, Brand, but when the dust settles maybe twenty minutes head start."

Simpson opened the back door of the livery. It swung wide on creaking leather hinges.

"How do you figure that, Wilbur?"

"I don't know what you done up there, but I heard a shot and then saw people walkin' toward the hotel. After I seen that flyer, I figured you was mixed up in it so I saddled your gelding. You run into them two hardcases?"

"Nope. A deputy marshal from Abilene."

"Uh-oh. You kill him?"

"Yeah," Jed lied. "Shot him plumb dead. A case of self-defense. He was aimin' to shoot me."

"You're in a heap of trouble, I'd say. I saw the flyer on you. Your name's Jed Brand. That's the name that other feller's usin'."

"I know. His name is Silas Colter, and he's the man who should be on that flyer, not me."

"Whoooeee, it don't look good, do it?"

"No." Jed untied Jubal and climbed into the saddle. "I appreciate any slowness you can talk that posse into."

"You figger a posse'll be comin' after you?"

"That's been my experience and my luck."

"Maybe not here. The sheriff's old and slow, and he don't like to ride beyond the town limits. He either goes to the army or he waits for a U.S. marshal to do his chasin' work."

"Well, somebody's going to be coming after me, old-timer. There's two more men from Abilene rootin' around town for me, and one of 'em's a gunslick name of Jellico."

"And you might have that Colter jasper after you, too, and those two waddies who rode in to meet him."

"Yeah, it might get pretty crowded wherever I ride."

Jed kept looking up the street. He saw people walking back and forth across the street but saw no horses coming after him. Maybe Ethan was spinning a yarn to the sheriff or the deputy marshals, trying to delay them from coming after him. Still, he knew he could not linger long.

"I'll be seein' you, maybe," Jed told Simpson.

"Hold on. I been thinkin'."

Jed turned Jubal, then reined him in. The gelding pawed the ground with his front hoof, and bobbed his head up and down.

"What?" Jed asked.

"You only faced one man back there at the hotel, right?"

"That's right."

"What if you run up against a passel? More'n one? All you got's that six-shooter and your rifle, that heavy old Henry."

"That's all I have."

"You need a Greener," Simpson said.

"What's a Greener?"

"A scattergun. Double-barreled. You stuff it with buckshot cartridges and you can cut down a passel of gunnies with just two ticks of your trigger finger."

"Well, I don't have a shotgun. Left mine at home, back down in Waco."

"I got one."

"Do you want to sell it?"

"I'd hate to see you come back here facedown, laid over your saddle, Mr. Brand. I kinda like you and I believe you got yourself into somethin' that wasn't your doin'. I've seen a lot of men ride through here and I got to where I could judge them pretty close. So, yeah, I'll sell it you, for ten bucks, and I'll throw in a couple dozen buckshot cartridges."

Jed was tempted. Simpson had a point. If he was up against more than one or two men, he'd be hard-pressed to defend himself. On the other hand, if he bought that Greener from Wilbur, he would be admitting something to himself that would forever be a part of his character.

He would be nothing more than a cold-blooded killer.

Jed felt time running out on him. But he knew he had to make a decision fast. And maybe he had to make more than one decision.

Both of them were a matter of life and death.

CHAPTER

17

J ED HESITATED, HIS MIND RUNNING AT A FAST GALLOP.
 Then he remembered something his father had told
him, something he thought he had forgotten in his bitterness over his father's abandonment of his family.

*When you come to one of those crossroads in life, and
you will, many times, be careful of the path you choose.
For each path you take will be a journey of your choos-
ing, Jed. Choose wisely.*

He sensed he was at one of those crossroads now.
And his father had been right. A man came upon many

such crossroads in life. He and Dan had taken one in Waco, when Colter made the offer to drive cattle up to Abilene. The wrong path? His father had told them it was not always easy to tell. But each decision carried consequences.

"Wilbur," Jed said, "thank you for the offer to sell me a scattergun, but I'm going to pass right now."

"It's sawed off and has a sling. You can carry it underneath your duster or a slicker and nobody would know it was there."

"I know. I'm just not ready to go that far."

"You got to figger the odds, Brand. You always got to figger the odds. And you're badly outnumbered from the looks of it."

"I know. I might could use a Greener, as you say, but. . . ."

"Whenever you're ready. The offer stands."

"Thanks. And, I'm not going to run, either."

"What?" Simpson cocked his head and looked up at Brand as if Jed had lost his senses.

Another path, Jed thought. Another crossroads in his journey through life. If he ran from the law again, he would never resolve the question of his innocence. But if he left Junction City, he would also miss confronting Silas Colter, and Colter was the only thing he needed to prove that he was innocent of those murders in Abilene. There were too many strings dangling in Junction City. If he were to leave now, he might never be able to pull a single one of them, or tie any of them into a neat, final knot.

"Is there someplace I can lay low, either here in Junction City or nearby? I don't want to be on the run all my life. That flyer has got it wrong. I never killed those men in Abilene. I never killed anybody. But the man who stole my name when he came here and traded horses with you is the guilty one. Silas Colter. He's coming back and I want to be here to meet him. He's the only one who can prove my innocence."

"Son, you got a hard row to hoe. You got the law after you and them two hardcases a-waitin' for Colter to put your gun against three. You add in the lawmen wantin' to take you back to Abilene and stretch your neck, and your odds of getting out of Junction City alive are like drawin' to an inside straight."

"Sometimes you can't figure odds, Wilbur. You have to play your hunch, and bet a bunch."

Simpson cackled, slapped his leg.

"Now, what about a place where I can hole up while this hand plays out?" Jed asked.

"You see that crick that runs through town?"

"Yes."

"That there's Solomon Crick, and if you go south of town a little ways, and head west, they's a little place used to be called Robber's Roost. In the old days, before the army come here, outlaws used to hole up there. Nothin' much left of it, a couple of sod houses and some walls. It's all growed up, last time I seen it, but you can see riders comin' from any direction for a long ways off. If I was to need a hidey-hole, that'd be it."

"Thanks, Wilbur. You keep that to yourself, will you? If a man named Talbot, Ethan Talbot, comes lookin' for me, you can tell him that's where I'll be."

"I can keep a secret."

Jed touched his pointing finger to the brim of his new hat and turned Jubal, then rode out of the stables. He looked up at the sky and got his directions from the sun. He kept the livery between him and anyone who might be looking for him and headed south. The creek wound through town like a twisting serpent, and once he was out of sight of Junction City, he headed west, across the prairie, into the unknown.

A herd of pronghorn antelope stood some distance away, watching Jed's progress across the prairie, their white necks flashing in the sun as they turned their heads or dropped them to graze, while a single sentinel stood guard. He saw no suspicious tracks on the course he was following, and when he spotted the ribbon of creek glistening in the sunlight, he was glad to see that his view was unobstructed for several hundred yards.

Jed followed the creek at some distance, always eyeing the ground for horse tracks or man tracks. But he saw none. The creek meandered, and so did he as he followed it north, west, and south. Jubal whickered and his ears stiffened, began to twist in a half arc. That's when Jed spotted what looked like part of a wall, barely visible behind tall grasses and brambles. His heart quickened as he rode closer.

A covey of quail flushed just in front of him and Jubal stopped and rocked backward on his haunches. The quail scattered and glided to landings in the grasses, leaving the lingering sound of their whirring wings floating on the air and in Jed's memory. He could have dropped two of the birds, he thought, if he had his shotgun with him. Or, as he mused ironically, if he had bought that scattergun from Simpson and had it loaded with birdshot.

Beyond the remnants of the earthen wall, Jed saw a sod shanty, looking deserted, with grass growing up to its windowsill. There was no glass in the window and the dark square of the opening looked slightly ominous. He glanced down at the ground, saw that he was on a kind of path, a path worn smooth by footfalls, a path that wound through the tall grass like a game trail.

But there were human shoe prints on the path. He thought, at first glance, that they might be sandals because they were flat and had no heel marks. Curious, his heart beginning to beat fast, he drew his rifle and laid it across the pommel. Then he saw another sod house off to his left, one that was crumbling, with part of its roof gone, the grasses that were left all brown and sere from the sun and wind, long dead from when they were first put atop the structure.

He halted Jubal and dismounted, thinking that he might present a target for anyone lurking behind any of the soddies. He held the rifle and walked Jubal along the beaten path. On his right, he saw still another small sod shanty that was returning to the earth from whence it came. The roof was gone, and the walls were worn down by rain and time so that there were no longer any windows, or any shelter from the elements.

Soon, Jed came upon another sod shelter, one much different from the others he had seen. While the grasses still grew up around it, there was new sod on the roof and he saw patches of darker earth on the sides, as if someone had taken mud and filled in some holes. He halted and stared at it for several seconds, listening.

"Hello," he called. "Anybody there?"

There was no answer. A slight breeze riffled through the tall grasses around him. He looked at a dark vacant window in the soddy and wondered if there was anyone inside.

"Hello?"

Again, no answer.

Jubal nickered, his rubbery nostrils distending as he sniffed the air. Then Jubal's ears flattened alongside his head, and his eyes widened as he stared at the empty building.

"What is it, boy?" Jed whispered to the horse.

In the silence, in the soft susurration of the breeze, Jed listened intently for any vagrant sound, any sign that someone inhabited the house or was hiding somewhere nearby. He waited and listened, but he heard nothing.

He drew a deep breath and started walking toward the sod house. Someone had been there recently, he knew that. The path branched off and one segment led straight to the front door, which was new and in a wooden frame. It was closed tightly and even had a latch, which looked new and freshly whittled from wood.

"Hello the house," Jed called.

Nothing. No reply. Nothing but the soft wind in his ears.

He dropped to one knee and cocked the Henry, sliding a cartridge into the firing chamber.

"You just hold right where you are," a voice called. "You cain't see me, Pilgrim, but I got my bead right on your scraggly face."

Jed let out a breath and ducked down. He heard a click from somewhere in front of him, but he could see nothing. Nothing moved. Whoever was there had him in his sights and that man was invisible.

Then Jed heard a metallic click. He knew what it was. It was the sound of a hammer cocking.

He felt as if he were just a heartbeat away from eternity in that terrible instant when the silence rose up around him like a shroud woven of the softest gauze.

A meadowlark piped in the distance and he saw a pair

of prairie swifts dart overhead, twisting as they knifed through the still air.

The sun beat down on him and Jed felt the sweat trickle down his forehead from under his hat brim.

His throat constricted in fear as he slid his finger inside the guard and caressed the trigger, ready to shoot at anyone who approached him in a menacing manner.

The silence stretched on until it became almost unbearable, a silence so loud it boomed in Jed's ears like the roar of a terrible thunder.

CHAPTER

18

THE VOICE SEEMED TO COME OUT OF NOWHERE. JED couldn't pinpoint exactly where it was coming from even though it sounded very close.

"You the law?"

"No," Jed replied.

"Stand up."

"How do I know if I stand up, you won't shoot me?"

The voice cackled. "You don't. But if you don't stand up, I'll shoot you dead where you are. And set that rifle down. Let me see your hands when you come up out of that grass."

Jed debated whether or not to put down his rifle. If he did, when he stood up, he would be defenseless except for his six-gun, and he would not be able to draw it fast enough to stop a bullet if the man wanted to kill him. But if he didn't show himself, he was liable to be shot dead right where he was squatting so ignominiously.

"All right," Jed said, "but don't shoot. I mean you no harm. I'm just looking for a place to lie low for a while. A man in Junction City sent me here."

"You come up real slow, sonny. Hands high."

Jed squeezed the trigger of the rifle slowly while he held his thumb on the hammer. He eased the hammer down to half-cock and set the rifle down. If he needed it, he was hoping he could dive down and snatch it up quickly. So he set it down very carefully, in the path, so that nothing would obstruct his grasp if he had to grab for it.

"All right," Jed said. "I'm going to stand up."

He stood up, slowly, holding his hands over his head, palms out to show that they were empty. He felt foolish. He also felt as if the next sound he would hear would be a gunshot. The last sound he would ever hear.

"Now, step away from that rifle. Toward the soddy."

Jed did as he was ordered. He was in the open, just a few yards from the sod shanty.

"Now, you just hold up there, feller, and with one hand, unbuckle that gun belt. Real slow now."

Jed dropped one hand to the buckle of his gun belt and worked the tongue loose from the hole. The buckle opened and the belt slid free. He let the rig slide down his legs to the ground, then lifted his hand back up.

"Now, you step thisaway, feller. Toward me."

"I can't see you."

"Same way you was a-goin' and no sass, now, hear?"

Jed took a few more steps before the man ordered him to stop once again. He was only about four or five paces from the shanty. A meadowlark trilled a melodic line from over by the creek as Jed waited for the man to speak again. The scents of grass, water, and mud wafted to his nostrils and he felt the sun warm his shoulders. He might have been back home on an ordinary day, waiting for Dan out in a field, except that he was sweating like a running horse and his stomach was fluttering with fear.

"Now, then, let's take a look at ye," the man said.

Jed turned his head slowly until he was staring at the back corner of the soddy where a short, stout man stood as if he had appeared magically out of the ground. The man held a double-barreled shotgun at gut level, the snouts aimed straight at Jed's chest.

"Who are ye?"

"Jed Brand."

"Oh, ho, yep, you sure as hell are, feller. Only, you

don't look none like your picture drawing. I seen the flyer on you, Jed Brand, and it looks like I got me a triple bloodthirsty murderer with a two hunnert dollar price on his head. Why, you're just a pup, young'un, barely dry behind the ears."

"You aim to collect the reward on me?" Jed asked, sweat streaming down his face and body.

The man's expression changed with a suddenness that surprised Brand.

Even through his scraggly beard, Jed could see the scowl on his face. His eyebrows, as bristly as a pair of soot-covered pipe cleaners, seemed to bristle as they arched over his glittering, porcine eyes. His pudgy nose twitched as if his nostrils were filling with a disagreeable odor. His tongue flicked out over cracked lips, a garish pink against the blackness of his tobacco-stained teeth and mouth.

"Me? Turn you in to the law for two hunnert dollars? Temptin' as that might be, the sheriff'd likely put me in the hoosegow right along with you, and we'd both be shit out of luck."

"Are you going to kill me?"

"What fer? Do you think I have no respect for human life, sonny?"

"Well, no. But, you're holding a shotgun on me."

"Friendship don't often spring up all of a sudden. I'm gettin' to know you, Jed Brand. Maybe you want to shoot me and steal my goods. Not that I have all that much, but I got a roof over my head and some peace and quiet down here on the creek. That's worth something. A hell of a lot, really."

"I'm not a killer, Mister."

"So you say."

"I say it because it's the truth. One of the men I'm accused of murdering was my own dear brother. A man named Silas Colter murdered them and made everyone think I killed those men."

"Silas Colter."

"You know him?"

"I knowed him once. He's a snake."

"What do you mean?"

"I mean the man was born to treachery. I mean he's a low-down liar and a deceitful man, not worth the powder to blow him to hell. He kilt a friend of mine in Lawrence, oh, it's been five years now, but I remember it. Shot him in the back and then finished him off with a bullet to the head when my friend was down."

"Why?"

"That was Colter's way of dissolving a partnership. Maybe the same as with you. What did you do for him?"

Jed told him.

"Yeah, that sounds like Colter. Well, you passed the test, Jed. You can bring your horse up, get your rifle and strap your gun belt back on. You got any grub with you?"

"Not much. Some hardtack and jerky."

"Well, I got plenty. If you like goat."

"Goat?"

"Antelope. But I got taters and onions and turnips and dried apples."

The man cackled and his beady eyes sparkled with a look of madness, as if he had suddenly become addled.

"You know my name, what's yours?" Jed lowered his hands very slowly. The old man aimed the shotgun toward the ground, took his fingers out of the trigger guard.

"Well, they call me Galoot."

"Galoot?"

He cackled insanely again, before answering.

"I keep tellin' folks that it's really Curmudgeon, but they call me Galoot. Like 'Old Galoot,' you know?"

"Funny name."

"Names don't mean much where I hang my hat."

"Where do you hang your hat?" Jed felt foolish. He wondered if Galoot was mad. Sometimes he seemed quite intelligent and well-spoken. At others, he seemed to go off the deep end into a state of craziness as if he drifted in and out of sanity like a man who has spent too much time alone.

"Why, all along the owlhoot trail. I'm a fugitive just like you, Jed. Now, get your goods and come on in out of the sun. This soddy ain't The Palace, but it's better'n nothin' at all."

And that was how Jed became friends with a man

who went by the name of Galoot. He put up Jubal in a
lean-to Galoot showed him, a place where he kept a
moth-eaten burro that was the color of a gray mouse.
There was water under the shed in an old barrel that
had been cut in half and tarred on the outside seams so
it wouldn't leak. He had cracked corn and wheat in an
old wooden trough. The burro was hobbled, and Jed put
hobbles on Jubal, carried his saddlebags, rifle, and
bedroll into the shanty.

It was dark and musty inside the sod house with its
earthen floor. He could smell the onions and the apples,
too. It reminded him of their storm cellar in Waco. The
place had that same kind of aroma and made him a little
homesick. A couple of boxes served as chairs and one as
a table. Galoot had food on shelves and in boxes. Jed
noticed that there were holes in the walls that served as
gun ports. He thought Galoot might have dug them
through the walls himself.

"Make yourself to home, Jed."

Galoot kicked a sturdy empty box toward Jed. Jed set
down his gear and turned the box over and sat down.
Galoot laid his shotgun down on an old rug, next to a
rifle. When he sat down, Jed noticed that he had a pistol
riding high on his belt, hidden by the vest he wore. He
hadn't noticed it when Galoot was standing up. The man
was well-armed. The rifle was a Sharps carbine and
looked well-cared for, the bluing very shiny and gleam-
ing with oil.

"So, you're on the run, Jed."

"I reckon."

"But you came here. How'd you find this place?"

Jed told him about Simpson.

"Sometimes we find good fortune in the hands of strangers."

"I'm finding that out, Galoot."

"How come you didn't put a lot of distance between you and the Abilene marshals? Why did you come to this place?"

"Colter. He's coming to Junction City. Meeting a couple of hardcases named Norton and Burns."

"And what if you see Colter? That's three against one."

"I want to bring him to justice."

"Boy, you are a caution. Justice? There is no justice in the world."

"He has to pay for what he did to my brother and those two marshals. I don't want to be running all my life."

"Well, you got big ideas, but I know Norton and Burns, too. Know of 'em. They're as hard as they come. They'd swat you like a fly. You got greenhorn written all over you, Jed. And they wouldn't blink an eye. Just like Colter."

"I can't just let Colter get away with murder."

"Besides him, you got the law after you."

"Now more than ever," Jed said.

"What do you mean?"

"One of the deputies from Abilene was shot and killed today."

"You kill him?"

"He was trying to kill me."

"Haw. That don't make no nevermind. So you got another killing to answer to, Mr. Brand. What else are you keeping from this old boy, eh?"

"Well, there's Hoyt, a deputy marshal and a hired gun. They're both looking for me."

"Who's the hired gun?"

"His name is Jellico."

Galoot sucked in a breath and he shook his head. Then he looked at Jed with burning eyes, eyes that bored into him and made him squirm inside as if he were under the harsh glare of a blinding light reflected from a mirror.

"Jellico," Galoot said, his voice hushed. "You might as well go and find yourself a rattlesnake for a pet, young Jed. If that man is after you, you don't need no other enemies. He's as bad as they come, and he's got more blood on his hands than a butcher in a slaughterhouse. I pray for your soul, young man. I pray for your soul."

Jed felt the room go cold and he felt that coldness in his heart.

What had he done to deserve this? Was there a way

out of his predicament? Jed didn't know. But everywhere he looked in his mind, all he saw was death.

And death was that cold in his heart. Death was that fear in his belly.

Death was Hoyt and Colter, Burns and Norton.

But more than any of those, death was a man named Jellico.

CHAPTER

19

GALOOT HELPED JED ERASE HIS TRACKS INTO Robber's Roost so that there was no trace of him anywhere near the hideout. During that first week, Jed learned a lot from his newfound friend, and gradually his nervousness at being on the run subsided. He wondered, though, if he was turning into someone he didn't want to be.

"Galoot?" Jed asked. "How do you get used to this?"

"Used to what?"

"Hiding out. Being on the run."

The two men sat in the shade under a cottonwood that grew along the creek. Galoot held a pair of binoculars in his hand. They, like his Sharps, were army issue. Jed wondered if he might be a deserter, but he couldn't force himself to ask. For the past two days, they had seen riders off the road, searching for tracks, they supposed, but none had come close to Robber's Roost.

"After a while, it becomes second nature. But not so's you drop your guard. You kind of develop what I call another sense."

"Another sense?"

"I think of it as that, yes. It's like there's a sense underneath all the others. You sleep, but don't sleep. You don't hear anything, but hear everything. You don't look at anything in particular and you see what is important."

"A sixth sense? I've heard of it. Never knew what it meant."

"Well, I don't know if it's got a number, but it's like it was when you was in school, remember? You'd feel like somebody was behind you, somebody you couldn't see was a-watchin' you and when you turned real quick, you saw somebody starin' at you."

"Yes. I've had that happen."

"Well, on the owlhoot trail, it happens all the time. You feel a shadow on you and you turn around. There's nobody there. But maybe way across the street, someone's comin' at you, and you know you got to run or fight."

"I don't think I could ever get used to living like that."

Galoot let out that brittle cackle of his, a cackle that always ended in a soft squawk.

"You get used to it, or you get locked up. Or you die."

"I don't want to live that way." Jed looked at the blue sky, the small white puffs of clouds skimming slowly across the skies like balls of cotton on a smooth blue ocean. "What put you out here, Galoot? What are you running from?"

"Ah, I almost forgot." Galoot laughed to show that he was joking. "No, you never forget. You live with what you done. You sleep with it. You go back to it in your mind and wish you had done something else at the time. But you realize you done it and you can't go back and you can't change nothing."

"If you don't want to tell me, you don't have to," Jed said.

"I know. I been keepin' it inside me a long time. Sometimes it helps to talk about it. I don't mind. Not no longer."

Jed waited. He drew in a breath and held it. He let it back out through his nostrils, out into the silence.

"I was in the army. Seventh Cavalry. I was married. I got sick on patrol and my platoon leader sent me back to the fort. I went home and my wife was in bed with the sutler. He drew on me and I shot him. He shot at me, but his bullet struck my wife. She died in my arms. They arrested me for murder, but I escaped before my court martial."

"But you shot in self-defense," Jed said.

"Not according to the army. And I killed a soldier when I broke out of the stockade. That's how I got away."

"And you've never been caught."

"No, but the army doesn't give up. They're hunting me."

"Why do you stay close to the fort here? Seems to me that you're making it easy for the army to find you."

Galoot laughed. "Sometimes you hide in plain sight. The army thinks I'd be as far away from an army post as I could get. They're not lookin' for me around here. Besides, here I can pick up all the gossip. I have a friend at Fort Riley. Once a month, we meet up."

"And you trust this man?" Jed asked.

"Yes. He's my uncle, on my father's side."

Jed wanted to ask Galoot his real name, but he had the feeling that he would be overstepping some boundary that Galoot had established. If Galoot wanted him to know his true name, he would tell him. And maybe someday, he would.

"You got a girl back in Waco, Jed?" Galoot asked him a few days later.

Jed blushed.

"Not really."

"Most men your age have a sweetie."

"Well, I don't." Jed felt uncomfortable, but he didn't blame Galoot for asking. His mother had asked him that, and Dan had teased him about it.

"I don't believe you," Galoot said.

Jed looked up and saw that Galoot was staring at him with those drilling eyes of his, eyes that bored right through him and burrowed deep into his innards.

"Well, there's a girl," Jed said. "A real pretty girl. But I've never asked her parents to court her."

"But now you wished you had."

"I just never could get up the nerve."

"Tell me about this gal, Jed."

Galoot's eyes softened and Jed began to relax. He had not thought of her since Abilene, but on the drive up to Kansas, he had thought of her a great deal. Constantly.

"Well, her name is Felicia. Felicia Stevens, and she lives on a little farm west of Waco. I used to ride over there just to look at her. From a distance. I liked to watch her wash clothes and hang them on the line when that west Texas wind was blowing, making all the clothes flap and whipping at her calico dress. Or I would ride by in the evenings and hear her playing the piano. I would look in the window. Her fingers were so graceful. They flew over the piano keys like fluttering birds, and sometimes, when she had the window open I could smell her perfume, the lilac water she used. And if she was sitting on the porch, knitting, I could watch her for hours and never tire of seeing her work the needles through the yarn. I think she's the prettiest gal I ever did see."

"Um, sounds like you're pretty sweet on this gal."

"I like her. I—I guess I pine for her sometimes."

"Did you ever talk to her?"

"Oh, when I'd see her at church, I'd say hello, mumble something to her, and once I saw her at a pie social and wanted to buy her pie, but someone else did, some old man. I don't think she even knows who I am."

"I reckon she does. 'Member what I said about someone starin' at you and you feel it? Well, she probably knows you're watchin' her and wishes you'd come up and sit on the porch with her, or help her hang her clothes on the line. You've got to make the first move, Jed. That woman isn't puttin' on lilac water to attract bees."

Jed thought about Felicia a lot after that talk with Galoot, and kicked himself mentally for being such a clodhopper, a tongue-tied, awkward, shy, clodhopper who didn't have sense enough to come in out of the rain.

Every so often, Galoot would leave Robber's Roost and be gone for a few days. He told Jed to stay there and sit tight. He said he'd find out what he could about Colter and Hoyt and Jellico. Meanwhile, Jed's beard had grown out so that his face was fully covered in silky, curly hair. He no longer remotely resembled the drawing of him on the wanted flyer. Whenever Galoot was gone, Jed grew very nervous and lonesome.

"Well, what did you find out?" he asked Galoot one day, upon his return from town. Jed had been gone from Junction City for over a month.

"Some things," Galoot said. "Just keep your shirt on, Jed."

Galoot had taken his burro with him and come back with foodstuffs, whiskey, and a newspaper from Topeka. When they finished putting up the staples, Galoot pulled out his pipe and lit it. Dusk was coming on and it was quiet, with only the throaty burble of mourning doves over by the creek to fill the silence and the far-off yap of a coyote to punctuate the stillness of late afternoon.

"Well?" Jed ventured.

"First of all, Hoyt went on back to Abilene."

"What about Jellico?"

"Dunno. No sign of him, but Hoyt rode back alone, with his tail tucked between his legs."

"Colter?"

"Colter's up to something. He and them two hard-cases are still in town, like they was waiting for someone. Or something."

"What do you mean?"

Galoot puffed on his pipe and drew in a mouthful of smoke, which he released in a long thin plume that shredded to wisps in the breeze blowing off the creek.

"Colter's bought himself a little dry goods store right smack-dab in the middle of town. The store's got big glass windows in it so that he can see everything on the street. And the store is right across the street from the Junction City Bank. Them two hardcases, Burns and Norton, work there. Only, there ain't no work. Colter's got a sign on the door that says Closed For Repairs. And he keeps the inside dark, so's nobody can see much of what goes on in there."

"You think he's planning to rob that bank?" Jed asked.

"I wouldn't be a bit surprised. But that don't bother me much right now. There's something else you got to know, young feller."

"What?"

"Do you know a man named Lester Amory?"

Jed shook his head.

"Well, he's staying at a little boardinghouse near the edge of town. He's rode up all the way from the Rio Grande Valley, just to see you."

"Me? Why?"

"I don't know. But my uncle knows the lady at the boardinghouse, the one who owns it. He stays there from time to time. She says this Amory is willing to pay a handsome sum to anyone who will bring you to him, or him to you."

"What do you think?"

"He's not the law. Lady says he's a cattleman and she knew him a long time ago. In fact, he's married to her sister."

"What is he, then?"

"He's a cattleman and he hates Silas Colter with a passion. But he's not talking to his sister-in-law, or to my uncle. He will only talk to you."

"That doesn't make any sense," Jed said.

"No, well maybe this will," Galoot said.

Galoot took his pipe out of his mouth and looked at it for a moment. Seconds ticked by. Finally, Jed could stand the silence no longer.

"What, Galoot? I'm ready to have a fit."

"He says he might be able to help you with the law, get them to drop the charges against you."

"How?"

"I don't know. But I think you ought to meet with him. Tonight."

"Tonight?"

"Yes. My uncle's bringing him here."

"Here?" Jed's jaw dropped.

"Amory will be blindfolded. So he won't know where we are."

"Damn, Galoot. Are you crazy? It could be a trap."

"Might be. He's coming alone. And one more thing. He says he's got a message for you."

"For me?"

"Yeah, from your ma down in Waco."

Jed let out a long sigh. He looked up at the sky, at the shadows stretching out from the sod house, at a hawk floating over the creek, its wings fixed in a long slow glide. Then he looked at Galoot and shook his head.

"Where'd you put that whiskey you brought, Galoot? I could use a taste right now."

Galoot grinned as dusk began to steal the light from the day and the sky in the west turned crimson as if the fires of hell were being banked by some unseen demon.

CHAPTER

20

JED HELPED THE MAN KNOWN AS GALOOT TACK BLANkets up over the windows of the soddy after lighting penny candles inside the single room. The flickering light flung their shadows on the walls as they moved around inside, shadows that danced and writhed like the stories told around an ancient campfire inside a cave.

"You wait here, Jed," Galoot said. "It's time for me to go out and meet my uncle, bring that Amory feller in here."

"Is your uncle coming here with him?"

"No. He'll stand guard some distance away."

"You don't want me to see him or meet him, do you? Your uncle, I mean."

"No. Not yet."

Galoot slipped out the door, leaving Jed alone with his thoughts. The frogs and the crickets had long since gone silent as the fingernail of moon rose high in the sky, casting a dull pewter light on the sawgrass, the gama, the grama, the bluestem, and the profusion of wild weeds that grew up around Robber's Roost with its forlorn sod dwellings.

He heard Galoot walk around the shanty, presumably to see if the candlelight showed through the darkened windows. Apparently, he was satisfied because Jed heard his footsteps recede as Galoot walked away to meet his uncle and the man bearing a message from Jed's mother.

He missed her. He wished he was with his mother now, listening to her low, scratchy voice as she spoke of old times in Kentucky, of her own mother and father, her brothers and sisters. Only she had come to Texas, with his father, leaving her family behind. And she pined for them, especially after his father left. Later, she learned they had gone to Tennessee and then to Arkansas where they all drowned in a flash flood that roared through the hollow where they lived near a town called Green Forest. In the shadows on the wall, Jed saw her shape as she sat in a rocking chair, her gray hair lit by soft golden lamplight, their cat curled up at her feet on a small round rug she had made from scraps of heavy cloth. He wondered how she was faring, all alone, without Dan there, or him, to help, to bring food, to tend to the chickens and cows, the goats.

After a time, Jed heard the soft pad of footsteps and his blood quickened. He stood up and waited in the center of the room, his hand on the butt of his Colt. It could be a trick, he thought. Maybe this Amory was a bounty hunter or a lawman using deception to find him. He wondered at himself, at the strangeness of the suspicions he harbored. For he had always been a trusting person, and now he was thinking like a criminal. Like a man on the run. Like a man in hiding.

"Jed," Galoot called, from outside the door. "Comin' in."

The door opened and a man stepped inside the candlelit room, a black bandanna tied around his head, covering his eyes. Galoot entered just behind him and closed the door.

"Just a minute, Mr. Amory," Galoot said, "and I'll take that bandanna off."

Jed noticed that Amory wasn't armed. He wore no coat, but only a blue chambray shirt, cotton trousers, a short-brimmed Stetson, crimped in front, dusty boots. His hands were those of a workingman, rough as tree bark, scarred at the knuckles and pocked with nicks and furrows. As the bandanna came off, Jed looked into a face without guile, a face bronzed by sun and scoured by wind. The man had hazel eyes that flashed with flecks of gold and green in the flicker of candlelight.

"Jed Brand," Amory said, holding out his hand. "I'm Lester Amory from down on the Nueces."

"I'm Brand." Jed shook his hand.

"Sit down, sit down," Galoot said, an amiable lilt to his voice as if inviting the two men to afternoon tea. "Les, you pull up a box right there. Jed, you know where to sit."

The men all sat and Amory leaned forward, looking into Jed's eyes.

"You don't know who I am, do you, Mr. Brand?"

"No, sir, I don't. I'm told you have a message for me from my mother."

"Indeed, I do. But first, let me tell you this. I have a ranch down on the Nueces River. I raise beef cattle. A man named Silas Colter contacted me a while back, saying he could sell my beef at top dollar in Kansas if I would drive them up to Abilene. Those cattle you drove up from Waco were mine. I own the Two Bar Seven."

"The Two Bar Seven?" Jed's mind was racing.

"That's right. Sound familiar?"

"Well, sir, the cattle me and my brother drove up to Abilene from Waco wore the Two Bar Eight brand on their hides."

"Do you know what a running iron is?"

"Yes, sir, but it's a crime to use one. And, I never have."

"I know you haven't. I sent three of my best drovers with that herd. I expected them back two weeks ago. When they didn't show, I rode up north to Waco and found out what had happened, both to my herd and my cowboys. They were good hands. Honest boys. Like sons to me, they were."

"What did you find in Waco?" Jed asked Amory.

Galoot was hanging like a trapeze artist on every word between the two men as the candles flickered and flapped their yellow flames. A light, susurrant wind brushed against the soddy, sniffing like a vagrant wolf at all the windows and the cracks in the door.

"There's a little town south of Waco called Belton," Amory said. "There, I found the bodies of my three hands. The constable took me to where they were found. He also showed me the running iron which changed the 'seven' in my brand to an 'eight.' In Waco, I learned that Colter had hired you and your brother Dan to drive the herd to Abilene."

"Dan and I didn't know any of that, Mr. Amory."

"I know. Your mother was very hospitable, very worried. Then Dan's body was hauled down to Waco. Your mother buried him last week."

Jed felt the sudden rush of tears spill from his burning eyes. His throat constricted, ached as if he had swallowed a firebrand. He broke into sobs, his body shaking, his grief pouring from him in a gush of weeping.

"I—I'm sorry," Jed said, recovering. He wiped his eyes dry with his sleeve and turned, red-eyed, to Galoot. "It hit me all at once, Galoot."

"There's things you got to ride out, Jed."

"I told Ellen, your mother, that I was going to try to find you and your brother when I first talked to her. Later, someone brought her one of those flyers with your name on it, offering a reward. Ellen was devastated."

Jed swore under his breath.

"She told me you were innocent, that you would never murder anyone, much less your own brother."

"That's true."

"I told her about Silas, and what I had found out about him in Belton and in Waco. The man has a long criminal record. We don't even know if his real name is Colter. He uses many names, apparently."

"He's here," Jed said. "In Junction City."

"I know that now. The army man who brought me to you told me. Tomorrow, I'm going to ride into Abilene and talk to Marshal Smith and demand that he arrest Colter for rustling and murder. I'll tell him you're innocent. I feel sure that you will be exonerated, the bounty on your head lifted and the charges against you dropped."

"Why don't you have the sheriff here in Junction City just arrest Colter?" Jed asked.

"That's a funny thing," Amory said. "Or, maybe not so funny. I spoke to the sheriff when I first rode in here, looking for Colter. But I also talked to a man named Hoyt when I was in Abilene, who told me he had lost your trail over here in Junction City. Hoyt told me the sheriff here was a friend of Colter's. The sheriff, Clifton Robinson, served with Colter and another man who's hunting you, a man named Jellico, in the Civil War."

"What? Do you mean Jellico and Colter are friends?"

"That's what Hoyt told me. And Sheriff Robinson, as well. Have you ever heard of a man named Quantrill, Jed?"

"No." Jed shook his head. "Who's he?"

Galoot cleared his throat and spoke up.

"You never heard of Quantrill's Raiders, Jed?"

"No. Never heard of him." Jed looked at both men, wondering why they both knew of Quantrill and he had never heard of the man. "Who is he?"

"Quantrill led a group of men, soldiers, who were stationed in Missouri. They raided Lawrence, Kansas, early in the morning after the war had started. They went in there about five o'clock," Galoot said, "and started shooting and looting and burning down the town."

"That's right," Amory said. "Quantrill and his men murdered about a hundred and fifty men and boys. Colter rode with them, and so did Sorel Jellico, Fred Burns, and Ralph Norton."

"I never knew that about Jellico and Colter," Galoot said. "I swan, it's a wonder Colter can even show his face in Kansas."

"Well, not many people know it. But Hoyt did and so did Marshal Smith. And, of course, Sheriff Robinson knows, because he rode with Quantrill, too. But they all had different names then, and they covered their tracks."

"How did you find out about Robinson?" Galoot asked.

"Bear River Smith told me when I was in Abilene. He said he had been doing some checking. Robinson went by a different name and Smith can't prove anything, but he told me to be on my guard."

Jed looked at Amory in confusion.

"It looks to me," he said, "like I'm outnumbered here. How big was this Quantrill's army?"

"About four hundred men," Amory said.

Jed hung his head in despair. He thought about Colter and now saw him in a different light. It reminded him of stepping on a cockroach in his mother's kitchen and then seeing hordes of them stream out of the woodwork, running in all directions. He had been a small boy then, but the sight of all those roaches terrified him.

Listening to Amory now brought back that same feeling.

Jed was, once again, terrified at what he was facing. One of the candles hissed and sputtered out, plunging part of the room, where Amory was sitting, into darkness. He could no longer see Amory's face and the man's silhouette had a sinister look.

Jed wondered if he could trust anyone anymore.

And that included Amory.

And maybe Galoot, as well.

CHAPTER

21

J ED FELT THE DARKNESS CLOSING IN ON HIM, PUSHING deep into his heart, into his mind. What had seemed fairly simple before, getting Colter, now seemed like an impossible task. He knew now he was not only facing Colter and his two henchmen, but a host of others as well, most of them as faceless as Amory was now.

"How can you or I, Mr. Amory, beat these men? They're all over the place, like cockroaches."

"I think we might have an ace in the hole," Amory said.

"What do you mean?" Jed asked.

"Cal Garner. He was one of the U.S. marshals that Colter murdered in Abilene."

"How does that help me?"

"Cal has a brother, Luke Garner, who's also a U.S. marshal. He should be in Abilene by tomorrow. And he and his brother Cal were both born and raised in Lawrence. Their father and another brother were both murdered there when Quantrill staged his raid. I think Luke will want to help."

"I know that story," Galoot said. "I always wondered if it was true."

"It's true, all right," Amory said.

"I haven't heard it," Jed said.

"It was just one of the horrible incidents that happened that day in Lawrence," Amory said. "But this one was truly horrifying and cruel. There were four men holed up in a house. Two of them were Cal and Luke's brother and their father. Jellico was the leader of the band of raiders waiting outside. They asked the men to come out and surrender. They said they wouldn't be hurt. They said they just wanted them to surrender. So finally, the four men and their women came out onto the porch. Jellico asked the men to step off the porch and follow him and his men to safety. The men got off the porch while the women stayed there. Then, without warning, Jellico and his men opened up and they shot all four men dead while the women looked on. Then

Quantrill's men rode away without blinking an eye."

Jed swore under his breath.

"So that's what I'm facing," he said. "A merciless bunch of murderers."

"Pretty much," Amory said. "But you just sit tight here with old Galoot until I get back from Abilene. Galoot, I'll be at the boardinghouse within the week. I may have Marshal Luke Garner with me when I come back."

"You tell my uncle that," Galoot said, "and we'll keep an eye out for you."

Amory got up from the wooden box he was sitting on. He reached into his pocket and pulled out a wallet.

"Jed, I'm offering a reward for Colter. Dead or alive. But in the meantime, I want to give you some money on account, just in case you run into him and put him down."

"Keep your money, Mr. Amory."

"Why?"

"I'm no bounty hunter."

"It would be honest money," Galoot said. "Deserving and all, if you get rid of Colter and his gang."

"No," Jed said. "I'm not a killer. I'm hunting Colter for killing my brother. But I won't take blood money. And that's that."

Amory put his wallet back in his pocket. He shook hands with Jed and wished him luck. Then he and Galoot turned and walked out the door.

"See you in a while," Galoot said.

Jed heard no more after their footsteps faded. The two men did not talk outside where the sound carried far on the night air. He stayed inside, thinking over all that Amory had told him. At least, he thought, there was now some hope that he might be cleared of the murder charges and no longer be a wanted man.

Galoot returned a short while later. He lit a lantern and snuffed out the candles. Jed watched him, wondering if he was ever going to speak.

"Well, did Amory and your uncle get off all right?"

Galoot sat down, a faint smile on his lips. He dug out his pipe and began to fill it from a pouch he took from his pocket.

"Amory told me to tell you that he gave your mother some money down in Waco, because she said you'd never take blood money."

"What?"

"Yeah. He told her he was going to offer you a bounty for Colter. Your ma said you wouldn't take it, so he gave her some, but she made him swear that it had nothing to do with Colter."

"That's my ma," Jed said, with a grin wide on his face. "She's got sand."

"More than that," Galoot said. "I'd say she's got plenty of character."

"She tried to give me and Dan some of that character. My pa sure didn't have any."

"You miss your pa?"

"I don't know. I don't think about him much. Just wonder about him, now and again. If he's still alive. What he's doing."

"Maybe you'll meet up with him one day."

"I doubt it. I don't believe he ever thinks of us."

"He might surprise you. Blood can run pretty thick."

"Not his," Jed said, a bitterness edging his voice. "Look, Galoot, I don't want to talk about that bastard no more."

Galoot was lighting his pipe. He raised both hands in surrender and touched the match to the tobacco. It caught fire and he pulled on the pipe, drawing smoke through it into his mouth.

"It's been an interesting night," Galoot said, leaning back against the sod wall.

"Tomorrow, I'm going into town. I can't wait no longer."

"What do you mean?"

"I mean, I'm tired of hiding out."

"You can't face Colter and his men all by yourself. That would be suicide."

"What is this here? Life? I feel like a rat in a tunnel."

"You're safe here, Jed. And Amory's going to help you get out of your predicament. Just sit tight. That's my advice."

"I have the feeling that Colter's going to get away. With all this going on, with Amory and that U.S. mar-

shal, Garner. He's going to get wind of it and light a
shuck."

"So, let him do it. Let the government handle Silas
Colter."

"You know, all that business about Quantrill and his
Raiders, and Lawrence. None of those men have been
brought to justice. Have they?"

"Well, no."

"So, Colter has been getting away with murder ever
since the Civil War. And the sheriff here is crooked. I
just don't trust the law anymore."

"Well, that's the way a lot of folks out west feel, you
know. The law isn't always evenhanded, Jed. And, that
old gal Justice, she's blind as a bat. But you can't take the
law into your own hands. Not by your own self anyways."

Jed felt his anger rising. Galoot was right, of course.
But that didn't make his situation any less frustrating.
He could just see Colter slipping away again, leaving
Junction City and covering his tracks. Leaving to steal
and kill again. And again.

"Colter thinks he beat me, Galoot. He thinks he can
get by with murder. It's about time somebody stood up
to that bastard and gave him what for. He needs to have
the boots put to him and horsewhipped while he's riding
out of town on a rail."

"Hell, they ain't tarred and feathered nobody in a
long time, Jed. As for horsewhipping him, you got to get

through Burns and Norton and Jellico, maybe Sheriff Robinson, to boot, if you're planning on dealing out any justice to Silas Colter. They's grave markers all over Kansas and Texas where Colter has been."

"I know, and it galls me. Anyway, I'm going into town. I've got a beard now and I won't draw attention to myself. I just want to walk down that street and look in that storefront and see the bastard."

"You're plumb crazy, Jed. Maybe you got cabin fever from bein' here with me so long."

"Maybe."

"Well, at least you'll sleep on it. Maybe you'll feel different in the morning."

"Give me a pull of that whiskey, Galoot. Maybe I can get some sleep. I'm so wound up right now, thinkin' about Colter, I don't think I could catch ten winks, much less forty."

Galoot dug the bottle out of a box of foodstuffs, and handed it to Jed. Jed pulled the cork and upended it.

"Easy now," Galoot said.

Jed handed the bottle back to Galoot.

"That's enough," he said. "I'm ready to hit the bedroll."

"Sleep tight," Galoot said, and continued to smoke his pipe. He took a swig of whiskey as he looked at Jed lying on his bedroll, his eyes closed.

Jed did not go to sleep right away. He lay there, thinking of Colter and what he had done to his brother, Dan. He thought about taking the law into his own hands, a law that had failed him and Dan. He thought about justice, too, and it all became raveled up in his dreams that night, and he dreamed he was running away from all of it and heading into a deeper darkness, a darkness fraught with peril.

And somewhere, far away in the dream, he heard the women calling his name. One was his mother, the other was a girl named Felicia Stevens. They both sounded lost and their cries tore at him, tore at his heart like the talons of some prehistoric bird flapping at his chest with its terrible wings.

CHAPTER

22

JED CARRIED WITH HIM THE TATTERED SHREDS OF HIS dreams, fragments of images that were disturbing as he ventured away from Robber's Roost. Galoot followed him on foot so that he could erase the tracks of the night before as well as Jubal's hoofprints.

"I still think you're a damned fool to go into town," Galoot said. "I sure as hell won't go to your funeral."

"Neither will I," Jed quipped, trying to erase some of the dread he felt.

"If you stay there, go to Norma's boardinghouse. It's

a log house near Simpson's livery. Mrs. Wilkins sets a fine table and won't wag her tongue 'bout you bein' there."

"Thanks. Is that where your uncle stays?" Jed asked.

"Lots of folks stay there. That's where Amory stayed."

"So, your uncle does stay there?"

"When the time comes, if you live long enough, Jed Brand, I'll tell you my real name. And my uncle's as well. If you start askin' a lot of questions at Norma's, she'll throw you out on your ear, most likely."

"I'll keep that in mind, you old galoot."

"Pshaw. Get on, will ye? I got tracks to sweep away."

Brand rode a roundabout way back into town, finally encountering small log houses and soddies that seemed to have been just stuck there on the edge, along the creek that flowed from the river that coursed through part of town. He felt edgy about sneaking in this way, as if he had done something wrong.

Jed knew what he had to do first, and he headed for Simpson's livery. Wilbur would know what was going on as much as anyone, and he felt he could trust him. It was quiet. There were few people on the street when Jed rode to the edge of town and rode Jubal up to the rear of the livery barn. Both the back and the front doors were open wide and he could see the entire length of the barn when he approached.

Wilbur stepped out of a stall as Jed sat his horse, looking for any signs of movement within.

"That you, Jed?"

"Wilbur."

"You growed a right bushy beard, I reckon. Recognized that horse before I did you."

Jed dismounted and led Jubal inside, through the liquid shadows bleeding from inside the stables.

"You might not want me to put that horse up," Simpson said.

"Why? What's going on?"

"Them three fellers come in here not ten minutes ago and saddled up, rode right into town like they knew where they was a-goin'."

"Who? Colter?"

"Yep, and them two hardcases, Burns and Norton. And, they were packin' iron like a gun drummer."

"Anything else?"

"Been a lot of people lookin' around since I last saw you. Askin' questions. The sheriff, for one. A hardcase name of Jellico, for another."

"You didn't tell them anything."

Simpson held up his arms like a seagull's bent wings.

"I didn't know nothin'."

"You're a good man, Wilbur. Anything else?"

"There's a new flyer out on you."

"Offering a bigger reward?"

"Wait here. I'll fetch it. It was brung to me by a friend of your'n, a man named Talbot Ethan. I seen him around."

"Was he lookin' for me, too?"

"He said if I was to see you, to tell you thanks."

Jed smiled.

Simpson went into the tack room. Jubal raked his front foot on the ground, pawing impatiently. Jed knew he smelled oats and corn and wondered why he was still under saddle instead of in a stall stocked with fodder. Simpson returned a few seconds later, carrying a flyer in his hand. He handed it to Jed.

"They got a beard on your face now," Simpson said. "Still don't look like you much. But this'un's a closer resemblance."

Jed scanned the flyer, reading it before concentrating on the sketch of his visage. The reward had gone up to three hundred dollars, but the charges against him now included the murder of Perry Boggs. He was relieved. At least Ethan hadn't been arrested and charged.

The sketch of his face was better than the first one, but his beard had grown longer. The drawing just made him look as if he hadn't shaved in two or three days. He handed the flyer back to Simpson.

"They didn't waste any time, did they?" Jed said.

"Took 'em about three weeks or so to get those flyers out. By the way, your friend Talbot told me something else. He said if I was to see you to tell you to watch out for Sorel Jellico. He said he's stalkin' you like a cat, all over town."

"Do you know Jellico?"

"I know him when I see him. He's been here, too. He's been all over. At the hotel, the sheriff's office, in and out of town. The man's a blood sniffer."

Jed wasn't surprised. He was only surprised that Jellico hadn't found him yet. He must not know about Robber's Roost, he thought. Or else he had seen no fresh tracks around it and never ventured into the area where the old sod houses were.

Sooner or later, though, he knew he would have to face Jellico. That was why he had been practicing his fast draw day and night while he was staying with Galoot. Galoot had approved, but only after he told Jed to file off the front blade sight from his pistol. He had to admit that his draw was a lot smoother now. There were no protrusions to hang the pistol up in the holster. Even though the sight hadn't hindered him, he could tell that without it, the pistol just fairly leaped into his hands once he snatched it by the butt.

"I guess I'd better skeedaddle," Jed said. "But I wonder if I could get a hatful of grain for Jubal here. He might need it in case we get chased out of town."

"Sure thing," Simpson said.

He started toward the sacks of grain stored next to the tack room, along with pails and nosebags. He was just reaching for a nosebag when shots erupted down the street. Simpson froze. Jed quickly led Jubal to the nearest post and wrapped the reins around it. Then he raced to the front of the stables. He heard Simpson's pounding feet just behind him.

More gunshots. Then they heard shouts. Jed and Wilbur looked down the street. They saw horses turning and rearing. Someone on horseback was firing a pistol.

"That's the damned bank," Simpson said.

"You sure?"

"I'm dead sure."

Jed stared down the street. Someone screamed. A man, from the pitch and tone of it, and there was more shooting. Then the man on horseback, who had been firing his pistol, wheeled his horse. He was joined by two other men. They were headed at a gallop straight toward the livery.

"You know who that is?" Simpson said.

"No. Who is it?"

"That's your man Colter and his two waddies, ridin' straight for us, hell-bent for leather."

Jed watched the riders, but they veered off, turned down a side street, leaving the main street empty.

"They're gone," Jed said.

"I saw 'em. They're ridin' here the back way. They'll pass by at the rear of my livery." Simpson was excited.

"I've got to stop them," Jed said.

"You can't go up against three of 'em."

"I don't care about those hardcases. Just Colter."

Jed started toward the other end of the stables. He

had not gone ten yards before two men appeared in the sunlit frame of the opening at the rear of the livery.

"You hold it right there, Brand," one of the men said. "I'm arresting you for murder in the name of the law."

The man who spoke was standing several yards in front of the other man who was in shadow.

"Who are you?" Jed asked.

"Sheriff Clifton Robinson. You drop that gun belt and walk towards me, Brand."

"Go to hell," Jed said.

Jed drew his pistol.

Simpson's mouth opened and his jaw dropped as he saw the quickness of Jed's draw.

Jed's big Colt cleared the leather. He thumbed back the hammer before the pistol was out of its holster. His actions were purely reflexive, born of constant practice until they were almost instinctive. He didn't think. He acted. He bent into a crouch and pointed the barrel of his pistol straight at the sheriff.

The sheriff fired at the same moment that Jed squeezed the trigger on his .44. Jed's pistol bucked in his hand. Fire-orange flame belched from the muzzle of his Colt and a cloud of thick white smoke billowed out, blocking his view. He heard the hornet whine of a bullet sizzle close to his ear and, out of the corner of his eye, he saw Simpson throw himself facedown into the straw and dirt on the floor of the stables. The sheriff's bullet whined off a metal object on the other side of the street, leaving a soft scream in the air as it caromed off in another direction.

Jed ran to his left, out of the line of fire so he could see if he had hit his target, the sheriff. The smoke from his pistol drifted away and he saw the sheriff down on his knees, clutching his chest. Blood spurted from a punctured lung and he made wheezing sounds in his throat.

"You ain't out of here yet, Brand," the other man said, stepping forward in a gunfighter's crouch.

Jed gasped aloud.

The man facing him was Sorel Jellico and he had already drawn his pistol.

Jed cocked the single action Colt and threw himself headlong into the scattered straw and horse dung just as a loud explosion filled the barn with its lethal roar.

CHAPTER

23

JED STRUCK THE GROUND AND PLOWED THROUGH straw. His elbows took the shock and he managed to keep his gun hand from striking the earth. After Jellico's pistol roared and spat lead at him, he heard the hiss of the bullet as it sped just over his head. Had he been standing, he would have taken the bullet square in his gut.

He tried to fix on Jellico, but the man was out of his crouch and bounding to cover, just inside the livery barn. Jed fired a shot at him, then rolled to his left, and crawled inside an open stall. He panted from the exertion and pulled himself up into a sitting position. He put the pistol on half-cock, spun the cylinder to the empty hulls, and used the rod to eject them. He stuffed two fresh cartridges from his gun belt into the empty chambers, and pressed the hammer into full-cock.

"You got three hunnert dollars riding on your head, Brand," Jellico called out. "I aim to collect it."

Jed said nothing. He was breathing hard, so loud he thought that surely Jellico would know where he was. He listened for any sound of movement from that end of the barn. He peered out through the cracks and saw Simpson still lying where he had thrown himself. Then Simpson started to crawl toward the stall where Jed was hiding.

"Simpson, you sonofabitch," Jellico yelled, "don't you move another inch or I'll blow a hole right through your head."

Wilbur stopped crawling. He turned his head toward Brand and Jed saw the fear in his eyes. They glistened with a wet light such as he had seen in frightened horses and cows. The look sent a shiver up Jed's spine.

Jed heard a gurgling sound that turned into a harsh rattle. When he peered through the slats of the stall in the direction of the sound, he saw Sheriff Robinson, still kneeling there, his body shaking with his death throes. Then, to his horror, the sheriff fell over on his side with a dull thud that echoed through the barn.

"Looks like you might have another hunnert or two on your head for that one, Brand," Jellico taunted.

Jed was beginning to get a picture in his mind about the killer he faced. From what he'd heard about him in Lawrence, with Quantrill's Raiders and what he was saying, the man must be unspeakably cruel. He sounded as if he enjoyed killing other men, even watching other men die. Again, Jed said nothing. He was not going to give Jellico anything to feed on. Not yet.

Jed heard the hoofbeats pounding close to the back entrance of the livery. Seconds later, three riders reined up, their faces covered with bandannas. He leaned out of the stall to get a better look, but not far enough to give Jellico a target.

"Sorel, let's go. Time's a wastin'. What in hell are you doin' in there? And where's Cliff?"

"You go on, Silas," Jellico said. "I'll catch up with you. Cliff's dead."

"I know that horse there," Colter said. "Sorel, is Brand in there?"

"He sure as hell is. It won't take me long to put his lamp out."

"Sonofabitch," Colter said.

Then, more hoofbeats.

"We got to light a shuck. Sorel, here's some of the cash. You know where to meet us."

Then Jed saw one of the riders throw a money pouch into the barn. It skidded a foot or two and landed near

Jubal, who shifted his weight and moved his rear end, spooking at the strange object.

"Brand, you ain't got much time. I can take you in alive. If you come out with your hands up and no weapon, I'll spare your life."

Jed would have laughed if he hadn't been shaking so hard with fear.

"Like you did those men in Lawrence," Jed yelled.

"You bastard. You don't know nothin' about Lawrence."

"I know you killed four innocent men in cold blood."

"Damn you. I'm tired of fooling with you. I'm coming to get you, Brand."

Jed pulled his head back in just as Jellico fired another round at him. The bullet chipped off a wedge of wood on the post and sent splinters flying. Some small ones stung Jed's face. His breath came hard again. He looked over at Simpson, who was hugging the ground as if trying to make himself even flatter than he was. Simpson was unarmed and Jed hoped Jellico would ignore him and not take his life.

He looked back through the crack in the stall. He heard movement, something that sounded like shuffling, like feet skating through loose straw. But he couldn't see Jellico. What was the man up to? He wondered.

It was quiet for a few moments. Then he heard the sound of rapid footsteps. When he looked, he saw Jellico running to the opposite side of the barn, toward the stalls there. He was hunched over, his pistol in his right hand.

Jed knew what Jellico was going to do. He was going to try and outflank him. He braced himself for Jellico's next move.

Jellico slipped into the farthest stall. Jed heard the door creak. It did not slam shut.

He stared straight at the stall. In the silence, all he heard was the buzzing of the horseflies he had not noticed before. They made a sound like bacon frying and some of them dove at his eyes and landed on his hat. He ignored them and watched that last stall, waiting for Jellico to make his next move.

Seconds ticked by.

Jed poked his pistol through a slat and rested it on the board. If Jellico showed himself, he was ready to tick off a shot. He aimed the muzzle directly at the stall door.

Sweat began to trickle out from under his hat brim, streak down his forehead and neck. The sweat made him itch, but he didn't scratch. The flies came at the sweat and he could feel their sticky hairy feet walking around on his skin. The waiting seemed interminable. The silence roared.

Then he heard the slap of wood, the creak of a board, the noisy clatter of someone scrambling over the whip-sawed boards that framed the stalls. He saw movement across the empty space between the rows of cubicles. It was too dark to see clearly, but he saw a shape slithering over the top of the last stall and then disappearing into the next. He knew what Jellico was doing. He was moving closer, stall by stall, so that he would end up across from him, with a direct line of fire into his stall.

The thin lumber would not stop a bullet. Jed knew that. If Jellico got into position and started shooting straight at him, it would be only a matter of time and a quantity of bullets before he was riddled with lead. He shuddered inwardly at the thought of being shot to pieces while he sat there, blind to his killer, helpless to fight back.

Again, Jed waited as the silence inside the barn swelled and became almost palpable. He heard the pounding of horses' hooves on hard ground and then saw a group of men ride by in front of the stable, down the street, heading out of town, presumably on the trail of Colter and his men. The riders were almost processional, seemingly not in any hurry to catch up with three armed and dangerous bank robbers.

That's when Jellico made his next move, scrambling out of one stall into the next one, coming closer to Jed.

Simpson made his move then. He got to his feet and duck-walked straight toward the stall that Jed was in. He moved fast and when he got to the door, he hurled himself inside, digging a furrow through the thick fresh straw.

"God," Simpson said in a low whisper as he turned over and looked at Jed.

"You should have picked another stall, Wilbur. Do you see what Jellico is doing?"

"I figgered it out. He's going to spray lead in here as soon as he gets in that opposite stall across the way."

Simpson pulled himself into a sitting position and scooted next to Jed, behind him so that Jed's body would block any bullets fired at him. Jed didn't mind. He would have done the same thing.

Jellico had two more stalls to go. It grew quiet again. Jed slid down, so that he was prone, presented less of a target. He pushed the snout of his pistol through the opening just above the bottom slat, aimed it at the place where he knew Jellico to be. Behind him, Simpson lay down, too, his breathing loud as he puffed for oxygen.

"Good," Jellico yelled across the way. "You both can damn well die in there. Simpson, you're a dumb sonofabitch."

Jed turned around, touched a finger to his lips, indicating that Simpson should not give Jellico the satisfaction of an answer.

"Brand," Jellico said, in a voice loud enough to carry across the gap between them, "you can still come out and save yourself. All I want is the reward money. Ain't no need for you to die over a few dollars."

Jed could not stand Jellico's lying. He kept thinking of what the man had done in Lawrence.

"Is that what you told those men in Lawrence when you talked them out of the house, Jellico? Did you tell them they could surrender and would not be harmed?"

"Brand, you should have been there. It was war. Yeah, you should have been there. Your pa was. He was right alongside of me on that raid. Didn't know that, did you?"

Jed twitched all over as if Jellico had rammed a knife into his belly and was twisting it. He winced as if he had been slammed in the mouth with a driving fist that came out of nowhere. His mind reeled and he felt a dizziness come over him as if he were about to faint.

His father? Was Jellico lying again? What did Jellico know about Jed's father?

"Shut your lying mouth, Jellico. My father was never in Lawrence. He wasn't a damned killer like you."

But the moment he said it, Jed knew that Jellico was telling the truth. And it made him sick inside, made him want to crawl up into a ball and hide from that truth. He was sick, and he gasped for air to keep from vomiting. The air inside the barn became foul and thick and the horse flies and the bluebottles swarmed at his face and dove for his eyes and he closed them to block out the hideous words still echoing in his brain.

Anger boiled inside Jed and tears scratched at his eyes like the gas from shaved onions. His hand gripped his pistol more tightly and his index finger began to slide along the trigger. He wanted to kill. He wanted to kill Jellico to shut him up and wipe out the lie about his father.

CHAPTER

24

JELLICO CLIMBED INTO THE NEXT STALL. HE MOVED TOO fast for Jed to crack off a shot. One minute Jellico was there, slithering over the top board like a lizard, the next he was gone, dropped down into the closed stall where Jed could not see him.

"Knowed your pa well, Brand. Your ma's name is Ellen, right? Yeah, old Jim used to talk about her a lot."

Jellico's words ripped into Jed's heart like daggers. His father. James Brand. If Jellico was lying, he was doing a pretty good job of it. His words hurt. Jed fought to bring his raging emotions under control. All of the years his father had been gone dropped away and he saw his face clearly in his mind. Saw his smile, heard his gruff laugh, saw him sitting at the table, making jokes with him and Dan, making his mother laugh.

True, his father had left home just after the Civil War began, late in '62, he thought. He might have been against the abolitionists, but Jed wasn't sure. Even so, why would he have gone to Missouri and joined up with Quantrill? It didn't make sense. And if he had done that, he must have had a very good reason. Was he like Colter and Jellico? Had he been that way all his life, and neither his mother, brother, nor he, had ever suspected that he had such a dark side? Jed wrestled with that notion but he only succeeded in complicating the puzzle even further.

"Don't let Jellico get your goat, Jed," Simpson whispered from behind him. "Don't pay him no nevermind."

"What if what he's saying is true?"

"Then there's nothing you can do about it. Lawrence was a long time ago."

"Brand?" Jellico again.

Jed stiffened.

"You're a damned liar, Jellico."

"I just wanted to tell you something, boy. That name you got is pretty fitting. Brand. That's what you got on you. A brand. The way you shot Robbie reminded me of your pa. Old Jim was a good shot, too. And as hard as they come

when it came to killin'. Yep, you got that same brand on
you, Brand. The killer brand. The outlaw brand."

"You don't know my father," Jed called out. "He's
dead."

"Oh no he ain't. He's alive and well, son. And, just like
you, he's ridin' the owlhoot trail."

Jed clenched his lips, the anger in him building into a
blinding rage. He turned to Simpson.

"Don't you have any horses boarded?"

"Nope," Simpson said. "Only had them three what
belonged to Colter and them other two, Burns and
Norton."

"Well, Jellico has two more empty stalls to go to
before he gets where he can see us plain through the
open door of this one."

"Yep. But, you can do the same as him. How many
cartridges you got on your belt?"

"I don't know. Sixteen. Eighteen, maybe."

"Just start making it hot for him in that stall where he
is. Maybe you can draw him out in the open. Just don't
waste all your bullets."

"That's an idea," Jed admitted.

It was something to do. It was better than sitting
there in that empty stall waiting for Jellico to get into
position where he could pick him and Simpson off like
turtles on a log.

"If I shoot at him, I'll draw his fire," Jed told Simpson. "You might catch a bullet."

"Might anyways."

"I like your attitude, Wilbur," Jed said with a wry grin. He felt the tension easing in him. Action was better than inaction, he reasoned. It would keep his mind off other things, and Wilbur could be right. If he fired into the stall where Jellico was, he might draw the man out. He could certainly make him think a minute before climbing over the wall into the next empty stall.

Jed drew a breath and slid his finger along the edge of the trigger. He looked for movement where Jellico was. It was so dark, he could see nothing. He tried to figure out where he might be inside that stall. In the center? Near the wall he planned to climb over? He didn't want to waste ammunition, but he wanted to try and shoot Jellico even if he had to do it blind.

Jed aimed the barrel just to the right of the center of the stall. He pulled the gun back from between the boards so the barrel wouldn't poke out. He would be shooting through boards. Maybe he could kill Jellico with a splinter, or at least, draw blood.

He held his breath and slowly squeezed the trigger. The Colt bucked in his hand as the powder exploded. White smoke burst from the muzzle of his pistol, obscuring his view. He knew that if Jellico was watching he would see the muzzle flash and have a target for his return fire. But Jed held his position and quickly cocked the revolver again. He slid the barrel over to the right a fraction of an inch more and fired once again. He heard the bullets smash into the wood and fracture the boards, splintering them as they passed through. He listened for a yell from Jellico, a sound that would tell him he had struck him.

"You hear anything, Wilbur?"

"Nope. You missed him."

"Maybe I hit him in the head and he's lyin' in there dead."

"Yeah, and maybe pigs got wings."

As if in reply to their wonderment, a shot rang out. Both Jed and Wilbur ducked. A bullet crashed into the stall, about a foot over their heads, tearing through the outer boards, showering them both with splinters. The bullet lodged in the back wall with a resounding *thwack*.

Jed raised his head slightly to look at the other stall where Jellico was. The door eased open as if Jellico had nudged it open with his foot. Then he appeared just inside the door, gun in hand.

"There he is," Jed breathed.

Jellico stood there, staring straight at him. Then he took a step and stood there, framed in the doorway.

"He's comin' out," Simpson whispered.

"He's hurt."

"Maybe."

Jed got to his feet. He stepped out of the stall, his pistol cocked and ready.

"You got lucky, Brand," Jellico rasped. His left arm

dangled at his side, the sleeve drenched with blood. "I'm still goin' to kill you."

As Jed watched, Jellico began to lift his right arm to point his pistol at Jed. It seemed to take a great effort. Jellico's arm rose very slowly and Jed thought his hand might be shaking.

Just for a split second, Jed thought about what he was going to do. He had already killed one man, but it hadn't sunk in yet. Now, he was about to kill another. He knew he could get off a shot before Jellico ever got his revolver level. Something his father had told him and Dan flashed through his mind in that split second.

"Don't never hesitate if you got to shoot a man who's tryin' to kill you," his father had said. "Don't even think about it. Just shoot. And shoot to kill."

No sooner had Jed thought of that when Jellico's manner changed, as if he had been transformed, brought back to life from the dead. Jellico went into a fighting crouch and his right arm came up like lightning. He seemed to lunge forward without moving and his pistol barked in his hand, spewing fire and smoke like a miniature dragon, the roar of it as loud as a cannon inside the barn.

Jed was already reacting when Jellico made that remarkable transformation.

As if some strange form of electric energy had ripped through him, Jed felt his fear vanish. His anger leaped to the fore in his brain, and he saw Jellico as the enemy, as a killer etched out of the background and standing stark and vivid before him. Jed charged straight for the gunfighter and the move probably saved his life.

As Jellico fired, Jed was running at full burst straight at his attacker, pistol held close to his side just above hip level. He seemed to startle Jellico, who struggled to cock his hammer a second time. His left arm dangled uselessly at his side, so he thumbed the hammer back with the thumb of his right hand.

Too late.

Jed ran up to him and fired point-blank into Jellico's gut. Then he fanned the hammer back with his left hand and, as Jellico stiffened in pain and tottered on the brink of eternity, Jed put his pistol inches away from the center of Jellico's forehead.

He squeezed the trigger and felt the kick of the .44 as it exploded in his hand. The bullet smashed through Jellico's forehead and ripped through his brain, turning it to mush. A rosy spray spewed from the back of Jellico's head as half of the back of his skull flew away like a china saucer. Brain matter exploded like balls of bloody cotton from the gaping wound in the back of the gunman's head. His eyes darkened to black agate and his face collapsed like melting wax.

Jellico's legs turned to rubber and he crumpled into a heap, his pistol still gripped in his hand as the muscles in his arm and wrist contracted. The acrid smell of smoke drifted up to Jed's nostrils, stinging the inner membrane. Without thinking he cocked the pistol again, the rage on his face like a red battle flag, flaring crimson as he stood over the dead man. Stood over him, ready to kill Jellico again.

And again.

Forever.

Even into eternity.

CHAPTER

25

JED STOOD THERE, STARING DOWN AT JELLICO'S LIFE-less body at the crumpled heap that had once been a living man.

The impact of what he had done was not yet clear and resident in his mind. It was as if someone else were standing there, an empty observer, caught for a moment in a timeless universe, suspended outside of the living world, a shapeless, thoughtless wraith floating on the edge of death, a place devoid of movement, of senses, of feelings. He felt hollow, drained, as if Jellico had taken some part of him into that netherworld of darkness where he had gone a few moments before.

What part of my life have you taken with you in death? What essence of my life have you stolen from me with your dying?

He looked at the small black hole in Jellico's forehead, the blown apart back of his head that was oozing brain matter like so much cornmeal mush.

Shoot to kill, his father had said.

Easy words to say, but when you blew a man's brains out, you blew away his breath, his body, his life, leaving nothing but a pile of rags covering an empty shell. The sightless eyes of the dead Jellico had grayed over and were fixed on some point of nothingness half a foot away, in the dirt and straw of the barn floor.

Jed felt a sinking sensation as if the bottom of the earth had dropped out from under him and left his stomach suspended in airless space and his thoughts spun around in his brain like a waterspout twisting across a foam-crested ocean. And then he felt as if he were standing on a vast empty plain, a place devoid of all life, deserted, abandoned under a black sky with a black sun hovering over a silent nothingness. In his ears, then, the soft roaring like the sound in a seashell, like a miniature wind sprung up from the spiraled ear of a hollow conch.

Simpson appeared by Jed's side. A hand touched his arm at the elbow as if to lead him back into reality.

"Jed," Simpson said.

Jed shook his head as if to shake out the desolate images inside, as if to bring himself back into a world where time existed, where things moved, where life flourished in the wake of a floodtide that had once roared across the land, sweeping all into its maw and leaving only silence and desolation behind.

"Huh?"

"You killed Jellico. I never seen anything like it. You run up on him and just blew his goddamned brains out."

"Shut up, Wilbur."

"What?"

Jed turned away from the dead man and headed for his horse like a man sleepwalking in the dead of night. He saw the money pouch lying on the ground and stopped. He slipped his pistol back into its holder, then bent over and picked up the pouch. There was printing on the side of the canvas bag.

Junction City Bank.

He shook the bag, heard it rustle with paper, and he knew that the paper inside was money. Stolen money.

Simpson walked over to the body of Sheriff Robinson, knelt down beside it and put a hand on his neck.

"He's turnin' cold. You sure enough—" Simpson stopped speaking when he lifted his head and saw the look on Brand's face. "Nothin'. Sheriff Robinson's dead, too."

"Wilbur, just shut up, will you?"

"I was only—"

Jed fixed him with a skewering look.

"Yeah," Simpson said, as he stood up.

Jed opened the canvas satchel, reached in and pulled out a wad of paper money. Simpson's eyes widened.

"Whooee," Simpson said. "That there's a heap of greenbacks."

"Stolen money."

They both stood stock-still as they heard galloping hoofbeats pounding outside, from both ends of the livery barn. Before either man knew what was happening, riders streamed in through the front doors, and through the back. Jed looked out at the backyard where Simpson kept a buggy, a wagon, a sulky, and an old harness. That's when he noticed a horse wandering around, its reins dragging. He had seen it before. It belonged to Jellico.

"Hold it right there," a man said to Brand. He was wearing a tin star on his chest and he had his pistol drawn and aimed straight at Jed. "Put your damned hands up."

Jed lifted both hands. One of them was filled with the wad of money, the other held the bulging bank bag.

"Looks like we got one of 'em," a man yelled from the front end of the barn.

Jed recognized some of the horses as belonging to the posse they had seen ride out of town not long before.

"Wilbur," the first man said, "stand clear of Sheriff Robinson. Is he dead?"

Simpson nodded, a dumbstruck expression on his face.

The man dismounted as half a dozen men leveled rifles at Jed from both ends of the barn.

"I'm Deputy Sheriff Earl Callan," he said to Brand, "and I'm arresting you for bank robbery and murder."

"Looks like you caught him with some of the goods, Earl," a man on horseback said.

Jed looked at Callan, who walked up to him and jerked the pistol from Jed's holster. He stepped back and looked over his shoulder.

"Lonny Lee, put the irons on this man. Don't he look like his picture on that wanted flyer? Yes sir, I'd say we got us a Jed Brand here. You Jed Brand, Mister?"

Jed nodded, then started to speak.

"But I'm not—"

"Shut up," Callan said. "I'll do the talking here."

A man came up behind Jed and pulled his arms down. Another snatched the bills and the satchel from Brand's hands. Jed felt handcuffs slide over his wrists as someone pulled his arms back until his shoulders hurt from the strain.

"He's Brand, all right," a man close to Jed said.

"Some of you men keep lookin' for them other three," Callan said. He walked up close to Brand and breathed bad breath on him from six inches away. "Your friends doubled back to get you, I reckon, or we wouldn't be so lucky to catch you, Mister Brand."

"They're not my friends," Jed said.

Laughter from the men surrounding the prisoner.

"We know you robbed that bank and now you've gone and killed the sheriff hisself. Barney, who's that other man over there?"

"His name's Jellico," Brand said, before the man could reach the body. "Sorel Jellico."

"He in with you on this? Why'd you kill him, too? I got you red-handed, you murderin' sonofabitch, and I'm goin' to claim that reward and see you hang before the week's out."

"Earl," Simpson said, finally, "Jed Brand didn't rob that bank. He was right here with me when it happened."

"Wilbur," Callan said, "you ain't got the brains God gave a piss ant. You just shut your flap until I can sort this all out. Barney, you and Lonny Lee and a couple of others take this man here to the city jail and lock his sorry ass up. Take his knife and check him for any other weapons he might have on him."

Brand felt himself being jerked away by men whose faces he could not see. He tried to fight back. One of the men brained him with the butt of his pistol. Jed staggered, his legs turning to rubber. The ceiling of the barn spun around as stars exploded in his brain.

Men pushed, shoved, and manhandled Jed down the

main street of town, straight to the jail. They took off the wrist cuffs and threw him into a cell that had two pallets on the floor. The iron door slammed shut on him, and the men who had brought him there left, closing the door to the office. Jed stood there, still dazed from the blow to his head, wondering how he was going to get out of still another date with the hangman.

Perhaps, he thought, Simpson will be able to tell Deputy Callan what happened at the livery and they would not charge him with killing either Sheriff Robinson or Sorel Jellico.

Those hopes were dashed several moments later when the office door opened and two men, one of them Callan, ushered Simpson into the jailhouse proper. The liveryman was not in irons. The other man unlocked the cell door and pushed Simpson in with Brand. Callan looked at Brand and scowled.

"You got a lot to answer for, Brand. I suggest you do some hard prayin' before you meet your maker."

Callan was whip-slender, with salt-and-pepper hair, wide-set hazel eyes, and thin lips that looked like a knife slash. His clothes were dusty and his shirt was soaked with sweat.

"Are you charging me with bank robbery, too?" Jed asked.

"Son, I'm chargin' you with damned near everything in the book. Including the murder of my boss, Robbie Robinson."

"You mean the man who rode with Quantrill's Raiders and burned down Lawrence, Kansas?"

Callan winced and his right hand shot to the butt of his pistol. For a moment, Jed thought the man was going to pull it out of its holster and shoot him right then. Callan's thin lips curled in a cruel smile.

"I'm goin' to enjoy watchin' you swing, Brand," Callan said. "I'm goin' to bring my whole family to watch."

Callan and the other men walked away and closed the door to the office. Jed heard voices rise and fall as the men conversed in the next room. He turned to Simpson, who was standing there, looking lost, a sad expression on his face.

"Why are you here, Wilbur? You didn't do anything."

"They think I was a acc—a—accomp—"

"An accomplice?"

"Yeah, they said I helped Colter and you rob the bank and—"

Simpson broke down in tears, and Jed felt sorry for him. He helped Wilbur sit down, his back to the wall. He squatted beside him.

"Don't worry, Wilbur, I'll convince them you had no part in any of this."

Simpson put his head down on his knees and continued sobbing, his body shaking. It was a horrible thing to hear.

Jed wondered if he really could help Simpson. From

where he sat, he didn't think he could help anyone, including himself.

He was a stranger in a strange town and there was nobody there who could help him.

He looked at Wilbur and wished he could cry himself. It might have made his situation easier to bear.

The talking died down in the next room and it was quiet in the cell. He heard people talking outside on the street, though. They were shouting his name.

And he heard something else that chilled his blood.

"Let's string the bastard up now," a man shouted.

And Jed knew he was talking about him.

CHAPTER

26

EACH DAY SEEMED LONGER TO JED THAN THE ONE BE-fore, with Wilbur whimpering on his pallet every night, two meals a day, cornbread, beans, beef, sometimes a turnip boiled white. Jailers came and went, taking each of them out separately for questioning by Deputy Earl Callan. Sometimes, Jed would see the wagons roll through town on the way to the railroad loading docks, their beds piled high with freshly picked corn, the ears unshucked and tasseled, looking like green insects held by tall wooden stakes and the smells of the corn and harvested wheat wafting into their cell were like the smells of freedom, a freedom denied them.

"They're going to take you to Abilene," Wilbur said one day.

"Where'd you hear that?"

"Hoyt come down with a court order. Seems Bear River Smith wants you to stand trial there before they bring you back here to hang."

"What about you?" Jed asked.

"I dunno. Deputy Callan says the circuit judge ain't due in from Topeka for another two or three weeks. There's all kinds of hell in Abilene."

"What do you mean?"

"Cowboys comin' up from Texas along the Chisholm, raisin' hell, tearin' up the town. Smith is mad as a wet hornet. A year ago, he took all the guns away from the cowboys and made all the whores move south of the railroad tracks. Did you know about that?"

"No. It was pretty quiet when I was there," Jed said.

"Abilene wanted the uncivilized element contained in that place. They called it the 'Devil's Addition.' That made the cowboys mad and they tore down all the No Gun signs and went on a tear. Now they're sayin' so many herds are comin' in, Abilene's gettin' wild again. I don't think you're going to find the judge or any of the lawmen in a good mood when you get back there."

Jed swore.

Where was Amory? He should have come back from Abilene by now. He didn't expect to get a fair trial there, and he knew he wouldn't get one in Junction City, either.

On another day, Simpson brought up Colter, as if he had been worrying the matter over in his mind for quite a while.

"You know that Colter was pretty slick, Jed," Wilbur said.

"About what?"

"Well, he knew he had a posse on his tail. He also knew you and Jellico were at my livery. And that you had already dusted Sheriff Robinson."

"Yeah. So?"

"So, he led the posse back to the livery. He also threw that money pouch at Jellico, and Colter knew it was there, too."

"Looks like he framed us both, Wilbur."

"Yeah, I been wonderin' how this all happened. You were right about Colter. He's a snake. I wonder where he went."

"Wherever he's gone, Wilbur, I'm going to get him. One day. Some day."

"If you live that long, Jed."

The cement floor of the jail cell had a drain. Jed and Wilbur pissed down it and the guard brought a pail of water once a day to wash away the excess urine. The cell still reeked of it all day and through the night. The jailer provided slop jars that were taken away and emptied every other day, so Jed had to endure that reek, as well.

At night, their cell was lit by a lamp in the hall outside, or sometimes, by a candle, again, on the wall beyond the bars. Jed would lie on his pallet and listen to Wilbur whimpering until he fell asleep, and then he would think of his mother, and home, and sometimes of Felicia, although her face was dimming with time, fading from his memory like a sun-washed tintype on a saloon wall next to a window.

On the third night of Jed's incarceration, a jailer entered the hallway and came to the cell door.

"Just wanted to see if you two were decent," he said. "You got a visitor, Brand."

"Who?"

"A lady."

A few moments later, the same guard escorted a woman to Jed's cell.

"Five minutes, Mrs. Wilkins," he said.

"Thank you, Gordon," the woman said.

The jailer left and the woman beckoned for Jed to come close to the bars. She was leaning on them from the outside.

"Hello, Mr. Brand," she said. "I'm Norma Wilkins. I run a boardinghouse in town."

She was a dark-haired petite woman with a pretty face, sharply angled, rich full lips, dazzling brown eyes, tiny feet. She wore a black dress with brocade around the bodice. A blue scarf was draped gracefully around her neck and dripped from one shoulder like a blue waterfall.

"I've heard your name, Mrs. Wilkins," he said.

"I was hoping to meet you under better circumstances, Mr. Brand."

"Call me Jed, please."

"Only if you call me Norma."

"All right, Norma. What brings you here to this dungeon?"

"Today, I received a post from Lester Amory, a former boarder. It was sent from Abilene. He asked me to get a message to you through a mutual friend I cannot name right now."

"I understand." He figured she was talking about Galoot. Or his uncle.

"Mr. Amory wants you to know that he has been delayed in Abilene and that he's expecting the arrival of a U.S. marshal named Lucas Garner any day now."

"Does he know I'm in jail?"

"I don't think so. You've only been here for three days. But I will inform him."

"Did he say why he was delayed?"

"He said he was trying to get the murder charges against you dropped."

"Did he say how?"

"No, I'm sorry, Jed. He did not. But he said he was optimistic, if that helps."

She made a moue with her mouth and stepped back from the bars.

"It helps. A little. I'm facing murder charges here, too, you know."

"I know. I'm sorry, Jed. I wish you good luck."

"Thanks. I'll need it."

"There's one other thing," she said. "Our mutual friend. He has to leave his roost, but he wishes you well."

"Trouble?"

"I don't know, Jed. He did not seem agitated. But I fear he has run into some trouble. He said something else, too, which I don't quite understand."

"What was that?" Jed asked.

"He said if you managed to get out of this, he hoped to meet you somewhere along the owlhoot trail."

"Thank you, Norma, but I hope I don't meet him along that trail. Right now, it doesn't look like I'll be anywhere but here in this jail."

"I believe Mr. Amory is trying to get you sent back to Abilene."

"Out of the fry pan and into the fire," Jed said, with a bitterness edging his tone.

The door to the office opened and the guard beckoned to Norma Wilkins.

"Time's up, Mrs. Wilkins," he said.

"Thank you, Gordon. Good-bye, Jed. I'll pray for you. I hope we meet again. Under better circumstances. My door is always open."

Before he could reply, she was gone.

Jed felt a sense of loss after she had left. He had smelled her faint perfume and the scent gave him a heady feeling. She also had brought memories of the outside world inside the jail with her, and now that she was no longer there, he felt empty inside. Empty, and all alone. He turned to see if Wilbur had anything to say, but even that companionship was denied him.

Wilbur Simpson was fast asleep on his pallet.

"Brand," the guard said, after Jed had been there for over a week. "You're goin' to Abilene after we wash you down."

"What about me?" Simpson asked.

"You're stayin' here until Deputy Callan says different."

"I'm innocent," Simpson said. "So is Jed Brand."

"Yeah, yeah, the jailbirds all sing the same old song, Wilbur."

Two guards took Jed to the river and made him strip. They tied ropes around his ankles and threw him into the Solomon River, dragged him underwater for a few feet, then hauled him out. He dressed and they took him to a waiting jail wagon, an enclosed buckboard with barred windows. He was put in shackles, the chains run through U-bolts attached to the iron floor and then padlocked. He noticed that they brought Jubal up, hitched him to the rear of the wagon. There were no other prisoners making the three-day trip.

The wagon was like an oven, but the days had turned cooler now that September was upon them. Jed looked out the window at the corn and wheat fields, and sometimes he'd see a farmer stop and wave to the two men driving the wagon. They stopped at noon for a meal of hardtack and beef jerky, peaches dredged from an airtight, and then did not stop again until the sun went down.

The guards, whose names he never knew, spoke little to him. They served hot food at night, which was beans and bannock, thin beefsteaks, and nearly rotten potatoes. He washed the food down with water. The guards took him out to relieve himself, but he slept in the wagon at night. In the morning, his bones hurt as if they had been pummeled with a constable's nightstick. He had shaved his beard, at Callan's orders, in the Junction City jail, but now it was growing back. And itching like ant stings. Dust spooled into the wagon through the rear window and Jed took comfort in looking at Jubal, who trotted behind the wagon on a manila tether.

The wagon pulled into Abilene in the dead of night. Jed didn't know what time it was, but from the glimpses he could get of the stars through one of the barred windows, he knew it must be after midnight.

The guards unshackled him and ushered him toward the jail. The jail he knew so well. Before he went in, under the softly hissing gaslight, he saw the gallows that had been erected in the middle of the street. He shuddered and a guard prodded him in the back, shoving him into the lamplit jail office.

"This here's Jed Brand," one of his guards said.

The jailer grinned with unconcealed glee.

"I knowed we'd get this rascal back," the jailer said.

"He's all yours. Just sign this paper. We'll put his horse and tack in the livery. Bob here has his weapons we took offen him."

The jailer took the large gunny sack that bulged with Jed's rifle, pistol, knife, and gun belt. The two guards left after taking off the iron cuffs.

The jailer drew his pistol.

"I hope you try to escape, Brand. Feel like runnin' right now?"

Jed said nothing.

The jailer was none other than Lloyd Hoyt. He raised his pistol, aimed it at Jed's forehead, and thumbed the hammer back.

The hammer made a harsh metallic click.

Jed did not close his eyes to wait for the explosion. He stared straight into Hoyt's black eyes, a look of defiance on his face.

It was the longest moment in his life.

CHAPTER

27

HOYT SLOWLY EASED THE HAMMER OF HIS PISTOL back down to half-cock. The look of contempt on his face remained fixed, as if frozen there.

"Move it, Brand," he said. "Through that door. You know where your cell is."

Hoyt waggled the pistol at Jed.

Jed opened the hall door and entered the cell block. Hoyt followed right behind him. The cell was open and Jed went inside. Hoyt pulled the door closed, took keys from his pocket and locked it. He holstered his pistol.

There were two men, presumably drunks, sleeping it off on the bunks.

"You got some company, Brand. Two Texas cowboys from Fort Worth. You boys are all alike. No respect for the law, a pack of drunks."

"What law, Hoyt? Yours? I didn't commit any crime."

"Haw. You're nothin' but a murderin' bastard. We hear you killed two more men in Junction City, one of them the sheriff. You'll swing at the end of a manila rope for those murders, too. Hell, we might even swing you twice."

Jed turned away. Hoyt's hatred of him was so thick he could almost touch it. He found a bunk, sat down on it. He lowered his head so he didn't have to look at the jailer. He was tired. His entire body ached from sleeping in the wagon. Light from a streetlamp sprayed through the window like a golden mist. Somewhere down the street a dog barked. One of the drunks was snoring.

He heard footsteps and when he looked up again, Hoyt was gone. A moment later, the door to the office slammed shut and he heard a key turn in the lock. He lay down on the bunk, folded an arm across his eyes and closed them. The cell reeked with the nostril-stinging stench of vomit, urine, and human sweat. Jed tried to ignore the smells and just drift off to sleep. But, though he was exhausted, his thoughts raged on like a millrace in the middle of a quiet stream.

Abilene. It seemed to be a curse for Jed. And for many others who came there. Like the two cowhands who shared his cell. Was it the end of the trail for him? He seemed unable to escape the gravity of this place where the first gun down had occurred. He felt swept up in some evil vortex that swirled at his legs and sucked him down into the depths of a maelstrom, unable to swim away, but tumbling and flailing his arms uselessly, kicking his legs like a galvanized frog and going back and forth between a rock and a hard place.

Finally, Jed sank into sleep, with none of his problems resolved, none of his questions answered.

The next morning a guard called Shorty came and let the two sobered cowboys out. Jed never did learn their names. Again, he was left alone until Shorty brought him coffee and a plate of stale beans, cornmeal mush, and rancid sausage that he couldn't swallow.

Around eight-thirty that morning, Bear River Smith looked in on him, but never said a word. He just walked to the cell as if to satisfy himself that Brand was in custody, and then left. An hour later, Shorty came in with Lester Amory.

"You got a visitor, Brand. I'll take your cup and plate."

Jed handed the dishes through the bars and, after Shorty left, Amory beckoned for Jed to come up to the bars where they could talk.

"Hello, Jed. Got yourself into quite a fix, haven't you?"

"I don't need a lecture, Amory. Fixes get me into them, not the other way around."

Amory chuckled.

"I have news for you, Jed."

"Good or bad?"

"All good, I think. Luke Garner is here in Abilene. He has been investigating the murders, and your story."

"Does he still think I killed his brother?"

"Not in light of other developments."

"What other developments?" Jed asked.

"Several. It turns out that Garner has been to Waco, investigating the murder of my cowhands. That's why it took him so long to come to Abilene."

"I don't see how that helps me."

"It turns out that there was a witness to Colter's murder of my men. A young man. Charlie O'Daniels. He saw the whole thing, and he had seen Colter before. Knew who he was."

"So, what are you getting at, Amory?"

"Garner let it be known at every stop on the way up here that this witness will testify against Colter in court. There are flyers out on Colter, offering a reward that I put up, one thousand dollars, dead or alive. The flyers mention O'Daniels and that he is a witness."

"Colter will kill him before he ever gets up on the witness stand."

Amory smiled knowingly.

"Exactly. Charlie is in Waco, waiting to testify when

Colter is brought in. Colter will know that by now. I expect he'll be going back to Waco, sooner or later."

Jed turned from the bars and paced to the end of the cell and back again. He stopped and looked at Amory.

"I still don't see how this helps me here. That gallows out there isn't a doghouse."

"Garner wants to talk to you, Jed. This morning."

"Why?"

"I don't know. But I have the feeling that he knows you are innocent. Not only innocent of the murders here in Abilene, but of those in Junction City as well."

"How would he know that?"

"He's a bulldog, that man. He's a tough, seasoned lawman. And he's smart as a whip."

"I'll talk to him, sure. But right now, I don't put much stock in the law."

"I know, I know. Here's the thing, Jed. If Garner can get you off, I want you to get back to Waco as soon as possible."

"You don't have to worry about that. I'm homesick and I'm sick of Kansas. Especially Abilene."

"When you get back, I want you to meet Charlie, stay close to him. Colter will show and I want you to kill him."

"I told you before, I'm not a killer. Especially not a killer for hire."

Again, that wry smile on Amory's face.

"You are now, Jed. Word is that you killed two men in

Junction City. In self-defense. One of them, at least, was a wanted man."

"Jellico?"

"Yes, Sorel Jellico. As for the sheriff, the word up here is that he was as crooked as a stick of mesquite. So those charges are going to be dropped, if they haven't been already. Garner will see to that, I think."

Jed shook his head. There were so many blind spots in what Amory was saying. So many ifs. Who in hell was Luke Garner? What could he do against a town that wanted his hide, that wanted him to dance at the end of a rope?

"You think, Amory. But you don't know."

"Have a little patience, will you, Jed? Garner has something up his sleeve. I don't know what it is, but I'm convinced that he believes you're innocent and that he can help you avoid a hanging."

"Well, where is he? Where's Garner now?"

"As a matter of fact, he's talking to the judge privately in the judge's parlor at his home. He told me that as soon as he's finished there, he'll come here to talk to you."

Amory reached into his coat and pulled two letters from an inside pocket.

"Garner brought these up from Waco for you, Jed," Amory said, poking the envelopes through the bars. "They're letters for you."

"Who are they from?" Jed asked, feeling foolish.

There was writing on the outside, names and return addresses.

"One is from your mother."

Jed took the envelopes, glanced at them. He was eager to read them, but not in front of Amory. In a way, he dreaded what his mother might have to say. And he didn't know who had written the other letter. He could not make out the handwriting.

"Thanks, Mr. Amory. Thanks a lot."

"Aren't you going to read them?"

"Not now. I'll read them later, when I'm alone. It might help the boredom of being in here."

"Look, Jed, I know you've suffered a hell of a lot being locked up down in Junction City and back in here. But you've got to show some grit. You can't let this jail wear you down."

"I'm trying my best."

"Good. I'm going out now to wait for Garner. He should be here soon. Just hang on, will you? Listen to the man. I feel sure everything's going to be all right."

"That's what my father used to say, Mr. Amory. Whenever anything went wrong, or we were having trouble, he'd say that same thing."

"Your father sounds like an optimist."

"Whatever that is."

"Someone who sees light in the middle of darkness. A man who believes in having hope, no matter how bad things get."

"Yeah? Well, I never believed him. It was just empty talk. Like everything else he said."

Amory cleared his throat in embarrassment, as if he were startled that Jed had let his feelings out like that, opening an old, raw wound that his father might have inflicted.

"Well, I'll be seein' you, Jed."

Amory walked to the door and knocked on it. Shorty opened and let Jed's visitor pass through. The door slammed and Jed heard the lock turn once again.

He walked to the bunk and sat down with the letters. His hands were shaking as he opened the one from his mother first. He recognized her crooked scrawl, the script from her tired old quivering hands. It was a short note, so he read it slowly to savor the joy the letter gave him.

My dear son Jed:

I know you are in trouble, but I pray to the Lord that you will be spared. I know you are innocent. I hope this letter reaches you up in Kansas. Come home soon. I'll bake you a pie. I cry for you and Dan every night.

Love,
Mother

Tears stung Jed's eyes and coursed down his cheek. He missed her. Missed her more than ever. He sniffed the letter to see if he could pick up her scent. She did not wear perfume.

But the letter smelled of flour and onions and sweet sorghum and the blossoms of flowers that grew in their yard. It smelled of honeysuckle and roses and the moon-flowers that grew along their fence.

The letter smelled of her, his mother.

And it smelled of home.

CHAPTER

28

JED FOLDED UP HIS MOTHER'S LETTER, PUT IT BACK IN the envelope and lay it on the bed. He picked up the other letter. But before he could open and read it, he heard the key rattle in the lock to the office door.

Bear River Smith stood by the cell door, along with Shorty, who carried a set of handcuffs with him, and the big ring with the cell key on it.

"Get your things, Brand," Smith said. "You're comin' with me."

Shorty unlocked the door. Sheriff Smith held it open as the jailer entered Jed's cell.

"Stand up and turn around," Shorty said. "I got to put these handcuffs on you."

Brand put the two envelopes inside his shirt, slipping them down the front. He stood up and faced the back wall. Shorty put the handcuffs around Jed's wrists. They snapped shut and Shorty spun Jed around.

"Walk," Shorty said, poking Jed in the back.

Outside, Smith took Jed's arm and led him into the office. A crowd of men stood there, all staring at Jed.

"Get out," Smith said. "All of you. Shorty, you stay. Lloyd, you come with me."

Jed saw Hoyt's face light up.

"Where are you taking me?" Jed asked.

"To see the judge, Brand. Just keep your mouth shut."

Judge Mordecai Harrison lived a few blocks from the center of the city in an imposing log house. To Jed, it looked like a forbidding place with its two-story structure looming over the humble cabins that lined the street. It had a cobblestone walkway and a large veranda. The door was oaken and at least three inches thick. Smith used the brass door knocker to announce their presence.

The door opened and a serving man greeted them.

"The judge is waiting in the parlor," the man said. "Follow me."

Hoyt and Smith flanked Jed as the servant led them into a room of stained-glass windows that sprayed colored light over the carpet and onto the leather chairs, the tables, and a divan encased in Moroccan leather the color of a rich maroon wine.

Two men waited in the parlor, both sitting in wing-backed baronial chairs. One man was small and bearded. The other looked as if he had been carved out of a chunk of the hardest wood, chiseled to a litheness, with burnished skin that bespoke of long rides in wind and sun, across desolate places. He was almost as tall as Jed and he had a silver shield on his vest that said United States Marshal. Cut into the shield was a five-pointed star of bronze.

The judge spoke first, his small mouth barely visible through his thick, wiry beard that seemed to sprout from his face like exploded wires of black, white, and gray.

"So, this is the infamous Jed Brand," Harrison said.

"It is," Smith said.

"He's tall, but from the stories I've heard, I thought he might be a giant."

Hoyt and Smith both laughed. The marshal did not.

"He's tall enough to hang," Hoyt said.

"Well, we'll see about that," the judge said.

"Anything else from us, Mordecai?" Smith said. "He should be in irons."

"That will be all, Tom. Marshal Garner and I will take

it from here. And, thank you for escorting your prisoner to my house."

"A pleasure, Judge," Smith said.

"Will you be wanting us to come back, sir?" Hoyt asked.

Smith shot him a dark look.

"No, Lloyd. If I need anything else, I'll let Sheriff Smith know."

"Yes, sir."

"Good-bye, Judge," Smith said, and turned on his heel. Hoyt followed him out. A moment later, Jed heard the front door close and the servant's footsteps vanished somewhere in the house.

"Sit down, Mr. Brand," Harrison said. "I just want to talk to you a minute before I let you and the marshal here talk between yourselves."

The judge pointed to a chair near the center of the room. It seemed to have been placed there beforehand so that it faced the two men sitting in front of the large bay window with its stained-glass portrayal of a hunting scene with Indians and buffalo somewhere on a sere plain.

Jed sat down in a straight-backed chair with leather trim. Everything in the room looked elegant to him. He had never seen anything like it.

"I'm Judge Mordecai Harrison, son, and Marshal Garner here has convinced me to write an order for your release into his custody. I believe he is going to escort you back to Junction City to face murder charges."

Jed's heart sank like a stone through murky well water.

"Luke here tells me that you are innocent of killing those two United States marshals and your poor brother, Daniel, was it?"

"Yes, sir," Jed said. "My brother's name was Daniel. We called him Dan."

"Are you innocent of those murders, Mr. Brand?"

"Yes, sir, I am."

"So you say."

"Yes, sir, I do say so. I would never kill my own brother. A man named Silas Colter killed him and those two marshals. And then he stole my gun to make it look like I did it."

"That's what Mr. Garner says. And I believe him."

"I'm glad to hear that, sir."

"All right, Mr. Brand. So far as Abilene is concerned, you are a free man. For the time being. The charges have not been dropped. To the outside world, you're still a man wanted for murder. Marshal Garner will explain the details to you more fully. I have issued an order for your release, and that is all. Do you understand?"

"Sort of. I guess." Jed squirmed in his chair. He didn't understand half of it. But he wanted to talk to the marshal.

The judge stood up.

"He's all yours, Luke. I wish Tom had cleaned him up before bringing him over."

"I'll take care of that, Judge."

The judge waddled out of the study and closed the door behind him.

The room grew quiet as Garner and Brand looked at each other, each assessing the other.

"I'll call you Jed," Garner said. "You can call me Luke."

"Yes, sir."

Garner smiled. That was the first sign of warmth or emotion Jed had seen in the seemingly stoical man.

Garner leaned forward in his chair as if to establish an air of confidentiality, and, perhaps, trust.

"Jed, what I'm about to tell you can go no further. It's just between you and me. Do you savvy?"

"Yeah. Keep my mouth shut."

"It's very important. I'm going to ask a great deal of you and I want your full cooperation. Otherwise, you go back to jail and face a meeting with the hangman."

"I understand. Luke."

Garner smiled.

"I want Colter. Pure and simple. He's been a thorn in my side for a long time. And you and I have something else in common. He killed your brother and mine. I want him as bad as I've ever wanted anything."

"Why can't you catch him? The law was pretty quick to arrest and accuse me. Colter's running free as a damned bird."

"I'll tell you why. Colter is slick. As slick as they come. He used you, as he's used many others in his career of crime. Just when I think I've got him dead to rights, he slips out of my grasp. He's one wily sonofabitch."

"I know that now. What is it you want me to do?"

Garner stood up and walked to the stained-glass window as if gathering his thoughts. He was tall and lean and broad-shouldered. For some reason, Jed had already started to like him. He seemed honest and straightforward. Garner turned away from the window and walked over toward Jed. He looked down at him, a look of concern on his face.

"Jed, the reason the judge didn't wipe out the false charges against you is because I want you to be a wanted man for a while. I want Colter to think he's gotten away with his schemes and these murders. Now I know you killed the sheriff in Junction City, and that's no great loss. He was a crooked sonofabitch and everybody knew it. Politics. It stinks to high heaven. And I know you killed Sorel Jellico. To your credit. He was a dangerous gunman and a wanted murderer."

"Yes, sir," Jed said, dropping his head like a penitent child.

"You did us all a service with the killing of Jellico. But that sheriff's death is going to hang over your head a while longer, too, I'm afraid."

"Why?"

"Because, Jed Brand, what I'm going to ask you to do

has to be done in secret. Just between you and me. Even Judge Harrison doesn't know anything about this. Neither does Tom Smith nor anybody else. And you cannot tell a soul, all right?"

"I guess so. What is it?"

"Jed, I want you to ride the owlhoot trail. I want Colter to think you're being hunted the same as he is. He might even ask you to join him. Now, I'll be following you and I'll give you help where I can. But you're on your own as far as Colter is concerned. And, as an outlaw, you must stay clear of the law at all costs. That means you're going to have to sleep in roach-infested flophouses, wander the West like a beggar, and act as if there was a price on your head."

"There is a price on my head."

"And it's going to get bigger. Starting today. Any questions?"

"Lester Amory thinks Colter is heading for Waco."

"So do I. And that's where you'll be going tomorrow. Now, I've got a hotel room for you, money, clothes, food for the trip. Your horse is out back, with your saddle on it, your rifle, and your saddlebags. I'll give you back your pistol when we leave here by the back way. You go to Waco, and you find Colter. I'll be right behind you."

"Will I see you there?"

"I don't know. If you find Colter, you will. Are you with me in this?"

Jed looked up at Garner's face, trying to read any

deception that might be in his eyes or on his features. The marshal was asking a lot of him.

"My mother—"

"Jed, you can't even tell her. From now on you're an outlaw. And only you and I know that you really aren't. It's got to stay that way."

Jed stood up when Garner offered his hand to seal their agreement. He stared at the outstretched hand for a long moment.

Finally, he shook it.

"Welcome to the Owlhoot Trail, Jed Brand," United States Marshal Lucas Garner said. "It's a lonely trail. It's a trail through hell."

CHAPTER

29

THE ROOM JED TOOK IN ABILENE WAS AT THE DRO-ver's Cottage, under a different name that Garner had registered him under earlier that day. He rode there the back way, his pistol in his saddlebags so that he adhered to Smith's "No Gun" law. There was a small livery in back of the hotel where he left Jubal, who had been glad to see him again. He gave the horse corn and oats, saw to it that he had plenty of water in his trough. He did not have to check into the hotel since Garner had given him his room key. Jed just carried his saddlebags and rifle through the back door and up to his room on the second floor.

He found new clothes there, and found that he could take a hot bath down the hall. When he undressed, the two letters fell out of his shirt. He picked them up and laid them on the bed. He wanted a hot bath more than anything.

When he took off his boots, he placed the money he had hidden there atop the bed and added the fifty dollars Garner had given him. He would be able to give his mother a tidy sum when he got back home. He had made Garner promise to see to it that Wilbur Simpson was exonerated in the bank robbery. Garner had agreed.

Jed soaked long in the tub, letting the heat from the water seep through his flesh to his bones. He felt the weariness wash away in the suds, along with the grime and dust that had covered him on the trip to Abilene in the jail wagon. He washed his hair, for the first time in months, and, after he dried himself, he started breaking in his new clothes, good denim trousers, a light chambray shirt, even new socks of woven cotton. When he was finished, he felt like a new man. Except he knew that he was still a wanted man.

He looked at the letters lying on the bed. He picked up the one he hadn't read yet, sat down at a table by the window and opened it, his senses bristling with anticipation as if the paper were magnetized.

He glanced down at the signature and his heart seemed to jump in his chest, skip a beat or two. He shook his head in disbelief.

Dear Jed:

 I saw your mother at church last Sunday and asked her where you were. I had not seen you sneaking around here in a long time. She told me that you were in jail, accused of murdering someone, including your brother. She said the charges were false and that you would be coming back home soon.

 I have missed you and I know you are not guilty of any crime. You are too sweet to kill or harm anyone. I know you have watched me. I hope when you come back you will ask my father if we can talk. We can sit on the porch or ride in his buggy some evening.

 I have been writing some poetry and trying my hand at painting. I like to do both. When I see you I will show you what I've been doing.

 I hope you do not mind that I'm writing you. Your mother, dear soul, said you would not. I just wanted you to know that I believe in your innocence, as does your mother, and I look forward to

*seeing you again. You do not have to sneak
around to see me or talk to me, dear Jed. I hold a
fondness in my heart for you, if I may be so bold.*
                                    Affectionately,
                                    Felicia

Jed's heart beat fast when he read the last words.
Affectionately. That meant that she liked him. And she
knew that he had been watching her from afar. Now her
face came back into focus. Reading her letter had made
him long for her once again and remember her sitting
on the porch, or serving supper to her parents in the
evening. He lifted the paper to his nose and sniffed it.

He closed his eyes and smelled the sweet perfume.
Lilacs, he thought. Some kind of fragrant flower. The
scent made his heart ache for her. Did he dare to see her
face-to-face when he returned home? He could offer
her little, or nothing. He was still considered an outlaw.
And he could not explain to her that he was really innocent and working for the U.S. government. He had
made a promise to Garner that he would not reveal their
arrangement.

He put the letter away and sat there, looking out the
window. He could smell the cornfields, picked clean
now, and see the wheat stubble all golden in the distance, and the cabins and dwellings of the town close by,
with people in them, strangers, Kansans who could not
read his heart or know that he was not a murderer.

It was going to be hard, he knew. Garner had told him that he would be chased, shot at, cursed, and hunted down like an animal.

Until he got Silas Colter. Only then would his name be cleared. Only then would he be free.

Jed left the next morning, before first light. He saddled up Jubal in the dark, with only a lantern for light, a lantern with the wick turned down low. The horse whickered the whole time Jed was cinching him up, pawing the ground with impatience.

"You know we're going home, boy," Jed whispered. "Don't you?"

Jubal tossed his head and snorted, his rubbery nostrils spouting a thin spray of steam.

Before Jed blew out the lantern, he saw a piece of paper on the ground. He picked it up and read it, a grim expression on his face. He folded the flyer and stuck it under his shirt. He wanted to look at it again in the daylight, when he was far from Abilene, heading south to Waco.

He rode out onto the deserted street. Somewhere, a rooster crowed and he saw bullbats with the silver dollars on their wings flapping overhead, snaring insects out of the air. As he rode beyond the town, past the wheat stubble fields, a gaudy cock pheasant flushed with a whirring of wings and sailed over the gray fields, gliding, finally, out of sight. His heart pumped with a feeling of exhilaration.

He thought of his mother and of Felicia Stevens. Both were waiting for him. That made him feel good.

He would not think of Colter yet. Not this fine September morning with the sun just beginning to push up over the horizon, lighting the far clouds with golden rays. After the sun was full up, and Jubal was walking at a brisk pace, his tail flicking at flies, he pulled out the flyer in his shirt and looked at it again.

He read the legend in bold black letters:

WANTED
DEAD OR ALIVE
FOR MURDER
JEDEDIAH "JED" BRAND

And, below the woodcut of his bearded face, there was more, and it was in a bigger type than the top part. Jed felt of his jaw. It was smooth and clean, for he had shaved off the beard.

REWARD
$500.00

Jed crumpled up the flyer in his hand and tossed it down on the road. Jubal shied at the wad of paper as it struck the ground.

Jed laughed.

"Hey, Jubal, I ought to turn myself in and collect the reward, give it to my ma. What do you think of that?"

Jubal whickered in his throat as if he understood.

Jed stood up in the stirrups and turned around to look back at Abilene. The houses had all disappeared. But he could see thin tendrils of smoke rising from the chimneys, thin and dark in the airless morning. And, soon, too, these disappeared as Jed and Jubal set forth that day on the Owlhoot Trail toward an uncertain destination.

ROUND 'EM UP!

THE BEST IN WESTERNS FROM POCKET STAR BOOKS

Cameron Judd

The Carrigan Brothers series

Shootout in Dodge City

Revenge on Shadow Trail

Cotton Smith

The Texas Ranger series

The Thirteenth Bullet

Gary Svee

Spur Award-winning author

The Peacemaker's Vengeance

Spirit Wolf

Showdown at Buffalo Jump

Sanctuary

Jake Lancer

Golden Spike Trilogy

Big Iron

Dusty Richards

The Marshal Burt Green series

Deuces Wild

Available wherever books are sold!

Visit
❖ **Pocket Books** ❖
online at

....

www.SimonSays.com

....

Keep up on the latest new
releases from your favorite
authors, as well as author
appearances, news, chats,
special offers and more.

SIMON & SCHUSTER
A VIACOM COMPANY
www.SimonSays.com